CF L515i

Lee, Robert C.

It's a mile from here to
glory

191056

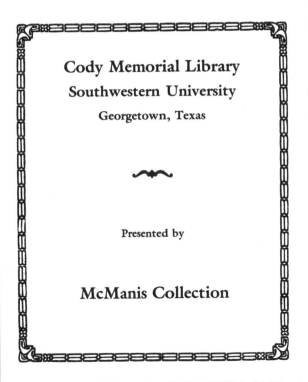

IT'S A MILE
FROM HERE TO GLORY

IT'S A MILE

FROM HERE
TO GLORY

by Robert C. Lee

Little, Brown and Company
BOSTON   TORONTO

LIBRARY OF CONGRESS CATALOG CARD NO. 72–170164

Sixth Printing

T03/72

MV

Published simultaneously in Canada
by Little, Brown & Company (Canada) Limited

PRINTED IN THE UNITED STATES OF AMERICA

To my mother,
who sometimes didn't understand—
but always tried

IT'S A MILE
FROM HERE TO GLORY

1

HE RAN ACROSS the meadow through the dead brown grass and over the wooden footbridge that spanned the creek. On the other side he veered sharply to the right and followed the worn path, the crisp sound of his hurrying feet blending momentarily with the soft murmur of the moving water. The old dry berry vines reached out and slapped against his trouser legs, their brittle teeth breaking against the tough blue denim cloth.

Abruptly, the path turned away from the creek and wound up the slope toward the top of the ridge. He pumped hard during the climb, the muscles in his short legs working into hard, straining knots. As he ran he flicked one hand repeatedly across his forehead and pushed back the long strands of red hair that kept tumbling down over his eyes. In his other hand he carried his school books, hugging them close to his body like a halfback racing down the field with the football.

"There goes Early agin," observed Arnold, the hired

3

hand. He rubbed his long tapered chin and made a little snorting sound. "Never seen that kid when he was awalkin'. Sure likes to run, don't he?"

Dave MacLaren paused beside the milk house and watched the tiny figure of his son far across the road. "Yeah," he said. "He's been running ever since he was a little kid. I guess he gets a kick out of it."

The hired hand turned and looked at his boss and then shook his head. He didn't understand. Why would a boy want to run all the time like that? Mighty peculiar. Furthermore, he didn't understand how a man like Dave MacLaren could have a son like Early. A big-boned, broad-chested man, Dave generally moved rather deliberately, walking with his heavy shoulders slightly stooped. His hair was black with just a trace of gray above the ears, and his eyes were dark and friendly.

Then there was his only son, Early . . .

Arnold shook his head again, shoved a fresh wad of chewing tobacco in his mouth, and went about his chores. For a moment Dave stood at the door of the milk house, his eyes a bit wistful and a trace of a smile barely curling the corners of his mouth. Then he sighed and went inside.

At the very crest of the ridge, Early paused for a moment. In the brisk morning air, his breath puffed out in steamy clouds. Despite the run up the slope, he wasn't really tired. He liked to stop here for a moment every morning because it was a good place to be.

Down below, the farm buildings were a sharp clean white against the brown land. The cows, fresh from their morning milking, moved lazily around the feedlot. Winter was almost gone and soon the grass would sprout again, jumping from the ground green and new. Only thin lines of dirty gray snow remained along the edges of the farm road where the tractor had piled it deep after the winter storms.

For a moment his eyes traced the path of the dirt road as it led south and bent sharply behind the shoulder of the ridge to meet the highway. That, of course, was the accepted way to get to the main road — by everybody except Early. His laughter at the thought erupted from his mouth like a jet of steam on the morning air. He liked to run the ridge, and for that, he supposed, there were those who thought him peculiar.

Well, nuts to them, he thought, as he turned and began to jog down toward the highway. He laughed again, and there was a trace of bitterness in the sound this time. If he was peculiar — then so be it!

Immediately upon entering kindergarten, Early Mac-Laren had discovered he was the smallest child in the class. He had never thought very much about his size before, but in school they just wouldn't let him forget. There was always measuring, pencil marks on the wall, big black-lettered charts for all to see, and vital statistics placed with great care in important-looking folders.

Early was also the smallest child in the first grade class the next year, and so it went right up through the grades. It was not a thing that gave a fellow much confidence. When he finally entered high school, it was even worse. The girls had always been big, but now the boys were getting big, too. Of course, Early grew along with everyone else, but never enough to close the gap with his classmates.

He was different. He sensed this not only in the attitudes of the kids at school, but also in the eyes of his father. When Dave MacLaren looked at his son and saw the bright red hair, the pale blue eyes, the army of freckles that merged into brown splotches across his cheeks, and the small, fine-boned body, he could barely keep from shaking his head.

"I'm a freak!" Early would cry bitterly. "I'm a midget!"

"You're *not* a freak," Dave would say in his big calm voice. "You're small, that's all. There's nothing wrong with that. Your mother was small and had red hair, too. You just take after her."

"It's all right for a girl, but not for a boy!"

"Look, Early," Dave would explain patiently, "a man is what he is. It's the inside part of a man that counts — not the outside."

But this was hard for a young man to appreciate. "I'm a freak," Early would repeat miserably, and with this the conversation usually ended.

Everyone has to compromise with his problems, and Early's solution was to keep pretty much to himself. The phone rarely rang for him in the evening, for he had few friends and most of them were younger than he was. On weekends and during vacations he helped his father on the farm. His schoolwork was generally acceptable, but never outstanding. Whenever he had the chance, he would do what he loved most — run. He jogged endlessly across the farm, his short legs pumping along like the pistons of a machine.

It was difficult to explain, but he knew that when he ran, he was ten feet tall. As he galloped across the fields, along the creek, or through the pine grove, it was as though he somehow entered a new dimension. Gone was Early MacLaren, the sixteen-year-old high school junior who stood a sawed-off four feet eleven inches and weighed a hundred and four pounds. Now he was a giant striding across a domain that was his alone. And sometimes he laughed out loud as he ran, because of the sheer exhilaration of it.

The path reached the highway, and Early slowed to a walk as he followed the graveled shoulder toward the bus stop at the mailboxes. The little drops of perspiration that had formed along his brow and on his temples evaporated quickly in the cool air.

The school bus appeared on schedule, and returning the driver's greeting with a nod, he found himself an empty seat halfway back, noting uneasily the presence of Jimmy Plummer in the seat directly behind.

Life had not been particularly kind to Jimmy Plummer. One of seven children in a family with little money, his face had been left partially paralyzed by a childhood disease. The outside corner of his right eye drooped, as did the corner of his mouth. On the rare occasions when he tried to smile, his face twisted into a grotesque caricature of the expression.

"Hello, runt," said Jimmy, with his usual unpleasantness. "How's Logan County High School's ace redheaded jockey this morning?"

A girl across the aisle turned and made a face. "He's uncouth," she announced to the bus. "Jimmy Plummer is uncouth."

Jimmy made a mock strangling sound. "Uncouth?" he squawked loudly. "Hey, you're wrong about that, Dorothy. All my friends tell me I'm real couth."

"Oh?" Dorothy's eyebrows soared. "I didn't know you had any friends," she fired sharply.

Jimmy winced and then leaned forward and placed a rough hand on Early's thin shoulder. "Old Early here, he's my friend," he said. "Ain't you, shrimp?"

Trying to ignore him, Early stared out the window, watching the brown fields rush by.

Jimmy gave the shoulder a painful squeeze and repeated, "I said, you're my friend, ain't you, Early?"

"What?" Early turned slowly and tried to be casual. "Oh . . . Yeah, Jimmy. Sure."

Releasing the shoulder at last, Jimmy leaned back and flashed his twisted smile. "Atta boy, Early. Early MacLaren — early worm gets the bird." He laughed vigorously for a moment and then suddenly he leaned forward again and said harshly, "Hey, runt! Where did you ever get a stupid name like Early anyway?"

And in a sudden explosion of action, Early vaulted over the top of the seat and began to whack his tormentor on the head with his geometry book. For a moment Jimmy cringed from the violence of the attack, and then he struck back. His right fist slammed against Early's shoulder, spinning him halfway around, but the redhead kept flailing with his book, catching the bigger boy over the eye with the edge of the stiff cover. A long red line appeared, and the blood began to flow.

The bus was in an uproar. The driver had stopped the vehicle and the kids were pushing each other to get a better look at the battle. Jimmy Plummer felt the warm blood dripping down from his eyebrow, and with an animal growl swelling in his chest, he wrapped both arms around Early and wrenched him clear of the seat. By the time the driver made his way down the aisle to them, both boys were struggling on the floor.

It was just after nine o'clock when the two boys entered the office of the dean of boys at the high school. In uneasy silence they stood before his desk, waiting for him to acknowledge their presence.

Quite deliberately the dean kept them waiting as he studied the report on his desk. At last he looked up slowly, his gray eyes, framed severely by black-rimmed glasses, studying first one boy and then the other. This was the dean's famed *look*, guaranteed to send tremors down the backbone of any student, from the smallest, greenest freshman to the biggest, most blasé senior.

He gave the paper before him several sharp raps with his index finger. "This is the bus driver's report," he said, displeasure quite evident in his voice. "I want an explanation, gentlemen, and I want it right now!"

"I was just settin' there mindin' my own business," blurted Jimmy quickly, "when this squirt here all of a sudden jumps over the seat and starts poundin' me on the head. Well, I —"

"That's enough, Mr. Plummer," said the dean sharply. Jimmy's right eye began twitching nervously. When the dean called a student "Mister," the boy knew he was in trouble. "I know you well enough. You've been a rather frequent visitor to this office." The steady gray eyes shifted to Early, and the man frowned. "But you — you've never been in here on a discipline matter before, have you?"

Staring intently at the floor, Early gave his head a slight shake.

"Tell me what happened," urged the dean. "Did you really attack him?"

Eyes still down, Early nodded. There was silence for a moment.

"Why?" questioned the dean finally.

"Well, he — he made fun of my — of my name," stammered Early.

"And that was enough to cause you to attack him?"

Early's eyes rose slowly until they focused on the man behind the desk. "I'm proud of my name," he said in a soft, steady voice. "My mother's name was Early — Mary Jane Early." His eyes dropped again. "She died when I was born."

Jimmy Plummer glanced quickly at Early, his anger suddenly gone. He blinked several times and swallowed hard. He hadn't known, of course, about the name. If he'd known, he wouldn't have . . .

The dean scratched the end of his long nose and pondered. "Well, under the circumstances, I suppose your reaction was understandable, Early," he said gently. He cleared his throat loudly. "Nevertheless, neither of you can be excused for your actions. Causing such a commotion on a school bus put the lives of every person on that bus in jeopardy. We simply cannot tolerate this sort of thing." He cleared his throat again. "Ordinarily, I'd suspend both of you, but the circumstances in this particular case are a bit unusual."

He got up to face them and was startled as he realized for the first time just how small the redheaded boy was. "Your punishment, gentlemen, will be twenty laps around the school track. In case you don't realize it, that's *five miles*."

He glanced at his records. "I see both of you are scheduled for physical education last period. You may begin running then and you'll continue until you have finished. I don't care if you run, walk, or crawl, but you'll complete those laps before you go home tonight. Do you have any questions?"

"We'll never be able to get them laps done during P.E.," protested Jimmy Plummer. "We'll probably miss the bus."

The dean gave him the *look* again. "That is certainly a distinct possibility, Mr. Plummer." He sat back down behind his desk. "That's all, gentlemen. You may go to your first-period classes, and consider yourselves very lucky. I don't want to see either of you in here again!"

In the hall outside the dean's office, Jimmy breathed a thankful sigh. "That was a close one, my little friend. Like the man said, we're lucky not to be out on our ears right now."

Early gave him a cold glare. "Don't call me your friend," he grunted.

Jimmy raised a casual hand. "Aw, come on. Let's forget the whole thing, huh? Look, I'll call up my old man and have him pick us up when we're through with them laps. It's a cinch we ain't gonna be finished in time to catch the bus."

"I will be," said Early as he turned and started down the hall.

Jimmy stared after him for a moment and felt his anger returning. "Sure you will, small-fry," he called. "You'll be out there pounding them sawed-off stumps of yours until the moon is out!"

When last period arrived, Early put on his gym clothes leisurely. By the time he reached the track, Jimmy Plummer had already completed the first of his twenty laps. Early jogged alongside the bigger boy for a moment.

"Well, shorty," panted Jimmy, "here you are. A couple of miles and those puny legs of yours will be worn down to the knees."

Without a word, Early stepped up the pace and pulled

away. His short legs set a rhythmic beat as he began the long grind. It certainly wasn't like running through the woods or across the fields, but it *was* running, and the joy of it filled him.

Ron Canepa, the picture of a young coach with his short dark hair, big square jaw, and sharp brown eyes that seemed able to observe a whole field of boys at once, was directing the physical education class. He fingered the whistle slung across the chest of his gray sweat shirt and shouted occasional orders to his charges. Satisfied that everyone was engaged in some profitable activity, he strolled over to the dean of boys, who was standing at the edge of the track.

"What brings you down to muscle alley?" grinned Canepa.

The dean returned the grin. "Just checking out a couple of boys, Coach. Gave them twenty laps for a scuffle on the bus."

Ron Canepa nodded. "Oh, yeah, Plummer and Mac-Laren. Heard about it. Well, listen, I'll keep an eye on them — make sure they keep going."

The dean raised an eyebrow as Early ran past them. "Doesn't look like we have to worry too much about that MacLaren boy. He moves right along, doesn't he?"

Silently, they watched Early run for half a lap, a frown growing on the coach's face. "Say," he said at last, "how long has he been running like that?"

The dean glanced at his watch. "Oh, he's been at it about fifteen minutes." He shot a look at the coach. "Maybe you ought to sign him up for your track team, Ron. Might make a pretty good distance runner for you."

"Arms tight and stride awfully short," Canepa muttered to himself, "but he sure does get it there . . ."

"Well, I'll leave them to you then, Coach." The dean turned to go and then looked back. "And, Ron — don't say I never do anything for the athletic department. Why, I'm probably the best talent scout on campus."

"Ummm, yeah," replied Canepa vaguely, too deep in thought to appreciate the dean's remark.

When Early finally finished his laps, he paused for a moment to watch Jimmy Plummer waddle miserably by him. Early had kept count as he passed the boy eight times. Poor Jimmy still had a long way to go, but Early felt absolutely no sympathy for him. He turned and started for the locker room. There was still time to catch the bus.

"Hey, Red," came a voice. "Hold up a second."

Ron Canepa walked over and grinned easily down at him. "How are you feeling, boy?"

"Feeling? I feel fine."

"Why, you're not even tired," observed the coach with surprise.

"I beg your pardon?"

"You've just run twenty laps and you're not even breathing very hard. You don't seem to be tired at all."

Early shrugged. "Oh, I'm a little tired," he admitted.

Hands on hips, the coach regarded the boy and then shook his head in disbelief. "I watched you. You kept up a pretty good pace all the way."

"Well, you see, I wanted to catch my bus," explained Early.

"You wanted to catch your bus," repeated Canepa slowly, and then he smiled. "You like to run, don't you?"

"Sure."

"Track practice began last week. Why didn't you come out for the team? We could use some more distance runners."

"Me?" Early pushed a fiery lock of hair out of his eyes and shifted his feet uncomfortably. "I — I don't think so . . ."

"Why not?" demanded the coach. "You said you like to run."

"Well — sure." Early frowned and looked uneasily toward the locker room. "It's — well, I do it for fun, you know? I mean — well, I'm just not good enough for that sort of thing."

"Why don't you let me be the judge of that," suggested Canepa.

Early shrugged. "Look at me, Mr. Canepa," he muttered. "I'm four feet eleven inches tall. The smallest guy in the junior class."

The coach nodded and placed his big hand on the boy's shoulder. "I don't care about your size, Early. Track is a great equalizer. It's not like football or basketball, where there's a premium on weight or height. Runners come big and runners come small."

"Yeah, but — "

"Lots of good distance runners are small," continued Canepa. "And I think there's a chance we can make a good one out of you."

For a moment Early met the coach's eyes, and then he looked away. "I — I don't know. I have to help my dad on the farm and I — "

"Well, of course, it's up to you. But think about it, Early, will you?"

Early nodded and edged away. "I'd better go, Mr. Canepa. I don't want to miss my bus."

Ron Canepa watched the small boy move toward the locker room, gave a deep sigh, and then turned away. "All right, Plummer!" he bellowed across the field. "Get up off that grass and get moving. You've still got a mile and a half to go!"

2

Early FORKED a pork chop out of the frying pan, helped himself to some mashed potatoes and peas, and sat opposite his father at the kitchen table. They ate in silence for a few minutes before Early said, "Dad, how much do you suppose a pair of track shoes would cost?"

Without looking up from the farm magazine he was reading, Dave murmured, "I don't know, Son." He continued to read for a few more seconds and then looked up abruptly. "Do you need a pair, Early?"

The boy shrugged. "Oh . . . I guess not."

"You going to do some running down at school?" Dave asked.

Early's expression was a bit pained. "I don't know, Dad. I might . . ."

"Look, if you need a pair of track shoes, Early, don't worry about the cost. We can afford it."

"I don't know yet," said Early. "I — I haven't really decided."

The next morning at school, he told the same thing to Ron Canepa when they met in the main hall. "Well, it's up to you," said Canepa. "Tell you what — why don't you come out and give it a try for a couple of days? If you don't like it, you can always quit."

"But I don't have any track shoes," Early alibied as he squinted up at the big coach.

"Oh, use your regular gym shoes for a while," smiled Canepa. "Then when you've decided to stick with it you can get yourself a pair of track shoes. And if it's a matter of money, Early, I'm sure we can — "

"No, that's not it," Early assured him. He sighed and finally nodded. "Okay, I'll — I'll give it a try, Mr. Canepa."

When he arrived on the practice field after school, Early found the sweat-suited members of the track team spread around on the grass doing various exercises. He felt uncomfortably conspicuous in his white high-top sneakers and gray gym shorts. For a moment he stood and watched a lanky Negro boy working out.

The boy looked up at him and grinned. "Hi, Red," he said easily. "Coming out for the track team?"

Early nodded.

"Well, you'd better start warming up or Coach'll get mad. He's a bearcat for warming-up exercises."

"When do we run?" asked Early.

The boy laughed. "Oh, we'll do plenty of that, don't you worry. First you've got to warm up, though."

Early spread his hands helplessly. "What am I supposed to do?"

"Here, try this one," the boy suggested. From a sitting position, he placed his left leg in front of him and curled the right one to the side. "This medieval torture is known as the hurdle split — among other things," he grunted, as he lowered his head until it rested on his knee. He straightened up again and nodded. "Go ahead and try it."

It wasn't as easy as it looked. The other boy grinned as Early got into position and made a face as he felt the painful tension wrack his calf and thigh muscles.

"Loosens up your legs real good. After a couple of weeks it won't feel so bad." They went through a series of exercises before the boy announced, "Well, let's jog a couple of easy laps now and we'll be all warmed up and ready to go."

"I guess we will!" exclaimed Early.

"By the way," said the boy, thrusting forward his dark, long-fingered hand, "I'm Billy Parnell. I've seen you around school, but I don't know your name."

"I'm Early MacLaren."

"Well, come on, Early. Let's get going before we cool off."

It took almost two of Early's small strides to match

one of Billy's long ones. Even so, Early felt quite comfortable running alongside the big guy. For once he seemed to be accepted for what he was — nothing more, nothing less. It would have been so easy for Billy to make some comment about his size or his name, but he hadn't.

They pulled off the track after jogging two laps and Coach Canepa walked over to them. "Hello, Early," he greeted. "Good to see you out. I noticed that Billy's been showing you the routine. That's good." The coach's big hand encircled the slim mahogany arm. "This fella's slow as an old toad, but he warms up real well."

Billy laughed and pulled away. "Okay, Coach. What do you say we go a quarter, eh? I'll even give you a fifty-yard head start."

"One of these days I'm going to take you up on that, Billy," the coach replied with a mock frown. "But I don't think you're in good enough shape yet for such tough competition." He turned to Early. "Seriously, though, it's important to get a good warm-up before you do any real running."

"Oh, I'm warm enough," Early told him.

"Good," said Canepa. His eyes narrowed thoughtfully. "I suspect that the mile's going to be your race, Early, but how about trying the eight-eighty today?"

"Eight-eighty?" questioned Early.

Canepa nodded. "That's the half mile, two laps around

the track. It measures out to eight hundred and eighty yards. Want to try it?"

"Whatever you say," said Early.

The coach smiled. "That's the spirit. My half-milers are due for a good workout." He turned and shouted, "Kramer, Church, Van Nuys! Get your sweat suits off."

Billy pulled Early aside, leaned down, and spoke to him in a low voice. "Watch out for Kramer," he advised. "He's the big blond guy and the best half-miler we've got. It might be smart to let him set the pace and just try to stay with him."

Uncertainly, Early moved to the starting line with the other three runners. He saw in their quick glances a mixture of surprise and amusement.

"On your marks," ordered the coach and the others dropped down into sprint start positions.

Early felt a surge of dismay. "Am I supposed to do that?" he asked unhappily.

"Just stand up and go when I say 'go,'" Canepa told him, and someone snickered. "Get set . . . Go!"

Away from the starting line late, Early immediately found himself behind the other three runners. The group remained bunched around the first turn, but as they reached the backstretch they dropped into a line with Warren Kramer moving out in front easily, the big blond boy running with loose confident strides.

Loping along behind the others, Early remembered Billy's advice as he noticed Kramer pulling steadily away up in front. Speeding up a little, Early caught the boy named Church about halfway down the backstretch, and by the time they reached the second turn he had moved up beside Van Nuys. The little redhead stayed there until they swung out of the turn, and then he moved alone into second place. The first lap was complete now, and Kramer floated ahead of him by ten yards.

"Atta boy, Red!" shouted Billy from the edge of the track. "Go get 'em, Early." He turned to the coach. "That little guy can really run, can't he?"

After a quick glance at his stopwatch, Canepa nodded. "Yes, he can," he agreed. "Doesn't look like much out there, but he certainly covers the ground." They watched as the second lap developed and Early slowly cut down the lead. "He'll never catch Kramer, though," he said.

True to the coach's prediction, the exhausted Kramer flung himself across the finish line a stride in front and almost collapsed as several teammates rushed to his aid. Canepa looked at his stopwatch again and grinned. "Two-oh-nine, Warren," he called. "Good job."

Hands on hips, Early walked slowly along the track. He was tired but far from exhausted. His head down, his chest heaving in heavy rhythm, he felt nothing but a bitter disappointment.

"What'd you think of the eight-eighty, Early?" asked the coach.

Early shook his head, eyes still down on the track. "Couldn't catch that guy," he muttered. He was silent for a moment. "I tried," he blurted suddenly. "I tried, but I just couldn't catch him."

Canepa regarded him intently for a moment, then slapped him on the back and chuckled. "Tell you what — in a couple of days we'll try you in the mile. Maybe that's your distance." The coach turned and headed for a group of boys working at the high-jump pit.

Early lifted his eyes and watched the retreating form. He felt hated tears of frustration building, and shook his head and blinked them back. A failure again. Shoulders hunched, he trudged slowly toward the locker room.

After dinner that night, Dave pushed back from the table and gave Early a questioning glance. "You're mighty quiet tonight, son. Something on your mind?"

Early shrugged and then drained his milk glass. "I've got some homework," he said in a low voice as he got to his feet. "Guess I'd better get to it."

"Wait a minute, Early," ordered Dave gently. "Sit down a second, will you?"

Slowly, Early dropped back into his chair. "What do you want?"

"Well, you were talking about getting a pair of track shoes," said Dave. "I was wondering if you'd made up your mind about it." He pulled his wallet from his hip pocket. "I'll give you some money and you can pick them up in town tomorrow. How much do they cost?"

Early picked up a fork and traced a pattern on the tablecloth. Finally he sighed. "I — I don't think I'll be needing them."

Dave tilted his head to one side. "Oh? Why not?"

"Well . . ." The boy sighed again. "You see, I ran today."

"How did you do?"

"I lost," Early replied quickly, and got up again. "You want me to clear the table?"

Blinking at the sudden change in conversation, Dave finally managed to shake his head. "No, I'll do it. You go ahead with your homework." After Early left, Dave poured himself a cup of coffee and for a moment he sat and stared morosely at the steaming black liquid. He took a deep breath and exhaled loudly through his nose. "This time," he said to himself, "I thought maybe . . ."

At practice the next day, Ron Canepa looked around and asked loudly, "Where's Early MacLaren?"

No one seemed to know. Several of the boys remembered seeing him at school during the day, but he certainly wasn't on the field.

"You want me to go look for him, Coach?" asked Billy Parnell.

Canepa shook his head. "No, Billy. It'd just be a waste of time. I guess he's quit, and we just don't have enough time to worry about him."

"But why would he quit?" asked Billy. "He did real well running against Kramer yesterday. I thought —"

"Billy, I'm a coach, not a child psychologist. Maybe the boy just can't stand to lose, I don't know. Now, let's get back to work, everybody!" he snapped.

With more than fifty boys out for the track team, Canepa had no time to waste on one temperamental redhead. Still . . . the kid sure could run. He gave an irritated grunt and headed for the shot area to work with the weight men.

The next day was Saturday, and Billy Parnell decided to spend the afternoon doing a little road work. His jogging brought him down the highway to a dirt farm road and a big oil-drum mailbox with black stenciled letters, "MacLaren Dairy." He hesitated a moment. Perhaps this was really none of his business.

Finally he made up his mind and started down the road toward the farm. Coming around the bend, he could see the house and the farm buildings ahead. There was a man working on the fence on the right side of the road. As soon as he saw Billy, he made an abrupt motion for him to stop.

"Hey, boy!" called Arnold. "Where do you think you're going?"

Billy stopped beside the man, feeling a flush of resentment at the insulting tone of the man's voice and the obvious distaste in his expression.

"This here's a private road, boy," Arnold continued. "Ain't just anybody can come down it. You got some business here?" he asked doubtfully.

Billy choked back an angry reply. "I came to see Early, Mr. MacLaren," he said softly.

The man blinked and continued to stare at him suspiciously. "I ain't Mr. MacLaren," he said finally. "I just work here." He jerked his head. "Early's out yonder in the pasture, bringin' in the cows. If you go out there, don't scare them cows none!"

Billy took a deep breath. "I get along just fine — with cows," he told the man. Then he turned and walked away. With easy grace he leaped across the strands of electric fencing and jogged across the pasture.

"Billy!" greeted Early with a pleased smile. "What are you doing out here?"

"Hi, Early. Just stopped to rap a little. What do you do, keep your legs in shape by chasing cows?"

Early laughed as he dashed about thirty yards to head off a wandering heifer. "Dad usually uses the jeep when he does this," he yelled. "But I kind of like to run."

Billy nodded. He watched the cows for a moment. The herd was moving slowly but steadily in the direction of the barn. "Seems like they know where they're going," he commented.

"Yeah," agreed Early. "You only get trouble from the younger ones. The old cows go in pretty much on their own." He squatted down, plucked a piece of grass, and stuck the stem between his teeth. "You have something special on your mind?"

"Sure," admitted Billy. "I want to know why you didn't come out for practice yesterday. Coach doesn't like guys who skip practice, you know."

Chewing on the grass, Early contemplated the parade of barnward cows. "Well, I wasn't really on the team or anything."

"I suppose you got your feelings hurt because Kramer beat you, huh?"

Early frowned. "Oh, I don't know," he mumbled as he got to his feet. "It just didn't work out, that's all."

Billy put his hands on his hips and shook his head with disgust. "Boy, what a king-sized inferiority complex you've got. I don't know why I'm wasting my time on a redheaded jerk like you."

Early flushed. "Something wrong with the color of my hair?"

Suddenly, Billy grinned. "Might look kind of funny on me."

Their eyes met for a moment and then Early laughed. "It might at that. Come on, I'll show you how we milk the cows."

"I know how to milk a cow," said Billy. "What I really want to know is, are you coming out for practice next Monday?"

"I wasn't planning to," said Early uncertainly. "You think I should?"

"Well, you shouldn't if you're afraid of getting beaten once in a while," replied Billy sharply. "But if you can spare me a minute, I'd like to tell you something."

Early leaned against a fence post and nodded.

"Well, one thing," began Billy, "is Kramer. He's one of the best half-milers in this part of the state. Last year he won the district championships in two minutes flat."

"Is that good?" asked Early.

"You'd better believe it is." Billy frowned. "You sure don't know much about track, do you?"

"Not much," admitted Early.

Billy shook his head. "Well, anyway, Kramer's a real good runner, and you really pushed him the other day. Besides, you didn't lose. You beat two guys, remember that. You did very well for the first time out — amazingly well."

"You really think so?"

Billy nodded emphatically. "But I don't see you as a half-miler. I think you'd be better in the mile. I'd like to see you come back and give it a try. Unless . . ."

"Unless what?" demanded Early.

"Unless you're too afraid of losing," said Billy quickly. "Early, my friend, every runner loses sometimes. You just can't win them all."

"Even you?" asked Early with the hint of a smile.

"Even me, man," Billy told him. "How about it? You going to give it another try?"

Early stared across the field for a long while without saying anything. Finally he turned to Billy and said, "You're right, of course. But I don't want to be a loser anymore. I guess maybe I just don't want to take the chance."

"Well, you can't lose if you *don't* take a chance," agreed Billy sourly. "But you can't win either, man. Now that's the important thing. A fella's got to win sometimes or he's nothing."

Early nodded slowly. "Well, I suppose since you've gone to all the trouble to come out here, the least I can do is —"

"Hey, whoa there!" said Billy. "Don't do it for my

sake, Early. Do it because you should — because you want to — or don't do it all."

Plucking another blade of grass, Early started toward the barn once again. "Whatever the reason, I'll do it. Okay? Come on, Billy. I want you to meet my dad."

3

Early RETURNED to the track team on Monday afternoon, but Ron Canepa gave no sign that he was aware of his presence. Early did some exercises, ran a few laps, showered, and then hitched a ride home. Tuesday was pretty much the same. Each time Early glanced in the coach's direction, Canepa seemed to be looking somewhere else.

So he was a bit startled when the coach came striding up to him on Wednesday just after he had completed his warm-ups. "Well, Mr. MacLaren, are you ready?" The words were cold and sharp.

"Ready for what?" asked the boy.

"To run the mile," snapped Canepa. "Think you can run four laps?"

"Sure," replied Early uneasily.

Canepa's eyes met his, hard and unsmiling. "That's fine." He turned and shouted, "Burdick, Howton, Joost, Carniglia, and —" He looked back at Early. "And MacLaren. Get ready for the mile."

Billy walked over and draped his long arm around Early's shoulders. "Here's your chance, Red. Coach'll put the first three across the line in the meet with Silver City this Saturday. Good luck."

"Thanks," mumbled Early, managing a very weak smile. "Any advice?"

Billy made a fist and punched him lightly on the arm. "Beat 'em."

"Runners to your marks!" barked Canepa as the five boys lined up at the start. "Get set." Everyone had stopped practicing and began to line the edge of the track to get a good view of the race. "Go!"

Early moved with the crowd to the first turn. *Just how fast do you go when you run the mile?* he wondered. The track crunched under his feet as he pondered. *Best to just stay up with the others. They know. They've done this before.*

Somehow he lost track of the laps. The five runners stayed tightly bunched and round and round they went. Suddenly the pace picked up noticeably. The quick burst for home caught Early by surprise, and the other runners left him behind. Desperately Early tried to overtake them, but with only two hundred yards to go, he was simply too late. With a tremendous final effort he managed to catch the last boy and cross the finish line a stride ahead of him.

Fifty yards down the track he stopped, put his hands

on his hips, and kicked unhappily at the track. "Fourth out of five," he muttered with great disgust. "A loser again."

"Well, what do you think, Early?" asked Ron Canepa, smiling at the little redhead.

"What do I think of what?" growled Early.

"Of the mile. Think that's your race?"

Early laughed bitterly. "My race? I did better in the half mile. Maybe that's my race."

The coach shook his head. "I don't think so. Look at you. You're not breathing hard at all." He scratched his big square jaw. "You know, Early, there are different ways to run the mile. You can loaf along for three and a half laps, like the boys just did, and then sprint like mad for the last couple of hundred yards. That's fine if you happen to have a real good finishing kick and the men in front haven't opened too much of a gap."

Canepa fingered the whistle around his neck thoughtfully. "Another technique is to go out and set a stiff pace all the way. Actually, the really top-notch milers do both. They set a fast pace, and they still finish with a good kick." He nodded slightly as he considered. "Yes, we're going to have to work on your sprinting a bit, but the important thing now is to concentrate on running those first three laps faster. I think you can do it." He smiled. "I *know* you can do it."

"What's the difference?" scowled Early, looking

down the track. "I finished fourth, so I won't be in the meet this Saturday."

Canepa raised an eyebrow and hid a smile. "Well, I wanted to talk to you about that, Early. You see, Carniglia, the boy who finished just ahead of you, is our best high jumper. This early in the season I kind of hate to have the boys double up if it's not necessary. So . . . if you're willing to give it a try, I'd like to have you fill in as the number-three man in the mile Saturday. How about it?"

Early looked up slowly, an uncertain expression on his face. "You — you don't think I'd make a fool of myself, Mr. Canepa?"

"Of course not, Early. I wouldn't use a boy if I thought that." The coach reached out and put his hand on Early's shoulder. "There's one thing I want you to understand, young fellow. I'm not thinking of you as a number-three runner, or a replacement or substitute. I really believe you have the potential to become an outstanding runner. Now what do you say to that, eh?"

"Well . . ." Early shrugged.

Canepa laughed. "Anyway, Early, I think maybe it's time for you to get that pair of track shoes."

Early waited until dinner was over that night and the dishes were all washed. "I'm going to run in the track meet this Saturday, Dad."

35

Dave blinked. "What did you say, son?"

"I said I'm going to run this Saturday so I've got to buy some track shoes," Early said quickly.

"Well . . . that's great, Early. Of course you can get track shoes. I already told you that. Say, what happened? Tell me about it."

"Oh, there's not a whole lot to tell. I'm going to be in the mile, that's all."

"That's all?" Dave laughed. "Listen, son, I don't know a whole lot about track, but I *do* know the mile is just about the most important race there is. What time is the meet? I sure don't want to miss it!"

"You — you mean you're going to come and watch?"

"Of course I am," grinned Dave. "You couldn't keep me away."

"But — but what about the cows and all?"

"Oh, Arnold can take care of them by himself for an afternoon." Suddenly Dave frowned. "Say, you do want me to come, don't you?"

"Well . . . sure. It's just —"

"Just what?" asked Dave.

"Well, Dad, I — I may not win, you know."

Dave leaned back in his chair and laughed. "Now we'll just have to see about that, won't we?"

The jersey was white with a crimson slashband that cut diagonally across his chest, and there was a big crimson "L" above the band on the left side. The jersey was much too large. The armholes revealed most of his ribs, and the tail hung almost to his knees. He crammed the excess material into his shorts, which were also far too big, requiring a safety pin on each side to cinch up the waist.

"It's the smallest uniform we got," grunted the team manager. "It'll just have to do."

"But suppose it starts to fall off while I'm running?" asked Early doubtfully.

"Well, you'll just have to hang on to it," advised the manager as he started to count a pile of towels.

"And look at the armholes," complained Early. "I'm practically naked."

The manager sighed and leaned on the pile of towels. "I *know* it doesn't fit, Early. We don't have a uniform your size. You'll have to make that one do."

It would do. Early stood by the edge of the track, his fingers tracing the big "L" for the hundredth time. Even if it didn't fit, there was a thrill in just wearing it and being part of all this.

"You ready, Early?"

Startled, he looked up at Ron Canepa. "Is it time already?"

"Already?" The coach smiled. The meet was almost over. The mile was the next-to-last event. For Early the afternoon had passed like a dream, with a carnival of people running, jumping, and throwing things. Now here was the coach telling him it was actually time to run. He couldn't quite believe it.

"You'd better get over to the starting line," said the coach. "Howton and Burdick are already there. And don't forget, Early. Get out there and run your own race. Don't wait around behind everybody else."

Nodding, Early turned and started numbly toward the track. Suddenly someone grasped his arm, and he heard Billy's voice say, "Luck, Red."

"Thanks," said Early, forcing a grin.

"And don't worry about the score," added Billy. "We got this thing sewed."

"Score?" Early blinked. Truthfully, he hadn't given a thought to the score of the meet. He wasn't even sure how the score was calculated. He gave a little shrug. Right now the important thing was the race *he* was about to run.

The starter glanced at Early, looked away, and then back again with considerable surprise. Could this little fellow be one of the milers? Well, he was wearing a Logan uniform and nobody was laughing, although the Silver City runners looked surprised too.

Early got a position well out from the poll as the starting gun was raised. He tensed his body, ready to burst away from the line and get in front of the pack. At the gun, however, he found himself floundering in a sea of elbows and flying spikes. By the time they reached the first turn, he was trailing the rest of the runners. *What a start,* thought Early unhappily. *What a rotten, miserable start!*

In the backstretch of the first lap, he swung wide and began a grim battle toward the front. He pounded past a couple of blue jerseys and a white one, and found himself in third place. Just as he finished the first lap he moved past another white jersey. Early recognized Burdick, Logan's number-one miler, as he moved by him. From the side of the track, Ron Canepa called the lap time: "Sixty-eight."

The first quarter mile in sixty-eight seconds. Early wondered if that was good or bad. The only thing he was sure about was there was still one more runner in front of him and he was wearing the blue of Silver City. Determinedly, he chopped into the lead, and halfway through the second lap, Early finally moved into first place.

A sports writer from Silver City nibbled on the eraser end of his pencil and raised his eyebrows. "Say, who's that little redheaded guy?"

The man standing next to him shrugged.

"He sure can pick 'em up and lay 'em down," observed the reporter.

The other man shrugged again. "They got a long way

to go yet," he grunted. "That kid'll never last. Too small."

Passing the starting line for the second time, Early heard, "Two fifteen."

Billy stood next to Canepa, watching the race intently. "So far so good, eh, Coach?"

Canepa nodded. "So far," he agreed. "Let's hope it didn't take too much out of him making up for that bad start."

The gap between Early and the second-place runner slowly opened to about ten yards and held there. The redhead seemed to move along without much effort. He didn't have the smooth gliding stride of the long-legged runners, but his short legs churned along with machine-like efficiency.

Trotting along the edge of the track as Early passed for the third time, Billy cupped his hands around his mouth and shouted, "Atta boy, Red! One more to go, Early." Early almost grinned. Obviously Billy did not want him to lose count of the laps, but today Early knew exactly where he was and how far he had to go.

"Three twenty-two!" yelled Canepa.

This was the lap that would tell, thought Early as he leaned into the first turn. Did any of those runners behind him have a big kick left? Maybe all of them did. He would soon know. How far back were they? He strained his ears but it was impossible to tell. He felt pain tug at his lungs and his thighs now, but it wasn't too bad.

With a half lap to go, Burdick moved up out of third place past the fading Silver City runner to challenge Early for the lead. Burdick gave it a good try, slicing the gap to a scant two yards as they swung the final turn and headed for home. Early was uncomfortably aware of the growing sound of footsteps behind him. Fifty yards from the finish, he couldn't stand the temptation any longer and sneaked a quick look over his shoulder. The glance broke his rhythm, slowed him slightly, and in that moment Burdick surged up even with him.

Stride for stride now, they stormed down the track. Ahead loomed the thin line of the tape. Just a few yards short of the finish, the pace finally told on the weary Burdick. Early's small chest parted the twine inches in front.

"Great! Great!" Billy was shouting in his ear. "I *knew* you could do it!"

Ron Canepa leaned down toward him. "Good boy, Early. Very nice race." He glanced at the stopwatch in his hand. "I caught you in four minutes thirty-one seconds."

Early blinked several times. "Is that good?"

Canepa grinned. "Not bad at all."

"I — I think maybe I can run it faster," said the boy.

"I know you can," agreed the coach. "And you will, too."

The sports writer from Silver City scratched his head and scowled thoughtfully. "Yessir, that little fellow can sure run."

"Too small," muttered the man next to him. "Never amount to much, I can tell you that."

"Well," said the sports writer, permitting himself a quick smile, "I guess I'd better find out how to spell his name, anyway."

Early woke to a bright new world the following Monday. For the first time that he could remember, he was anxious to get to school. "Gonna be a good day," he told himself happily. He smiled in the bathroom mirror as he dug a comb through his thick red hair. It was a useless effort, for the hair wouldn't stay combed very long, but the mirror smiled back.

That morning as he ran the ridge to the bus stop, the air seemed especially fine. He reran the race of last Saturday, bursting in front of the imaginary pack and blazing to a great victory as he reached the road.

He puffed a bit as he walked toward the mailboxes. His imagination had carried him away, causing him to run harder than usual. He leaned against a mailbox and smiled. It *was* going to be a good day. Heck, it was going to be a *great* day.

The bus appeared right on schedule and the driver gave Early a special smile of greeting. "Nice race last Saturday, Early."

Early felt a warm glow of pride mixed with some embarrassment, and he mumbled his thanks. It would not do to appear conceited, he realized. He wanted to seem casual about the whole thing, but that wasn't easy for him; he had waited such a long time for success.

Early found a seat, and Dorothy leaned across the aisle and flashed a dazzling smile. "It was thrilling, Early. Just thrilling."

"It was thrilling, Early," echoed a mocking falsetto voice from behind him. "*Just thrilling.*"

Early turned and met the twisted smirk of Jimmy Plummer. "Well, runt," continued Jimmy, "I understand you're the big track hero now. Tell me, what horse are you riding this week?"

Turning away, Early stared deliberately out the window, trying to ignore his tormentor. His perfect day was beginning to get a little cloudy. Perhaps if he didn't pay any attention . . .

But Jimmy was not easily discouraged. "You don't have very much to say, midget. What are you doing — counting your Olympic gold medals already?"

Sighing, Early turned slowly to face the big boy. "Cool it," he said softly. "We got in trouble on the bus once before. Remember?"

Satisfied that his barbs had reached home, Jimmy Plummer leaned back in his seat, folded his arms, and flashed his crooked grin. Then in a low voice he said, "Early MacLaren — world's greatest redheaded midget runner. The runner with the world's stupidest name: Squirrelly Early MacLaren."

The explosion that followed was even more violent than the earlier encounter. This time Early didn't bother with his geometry book; he used his fists. Though Plummer was half expecting the attack, Early landed his first shot right smack on his nose, drawing a howl that was a combination of pain and rage. Jimmy retaliated immediately, his roundhouse right blasting Early clear out into the aisle.

In another moment they were down on the floor between the rows of seats. By the time the angry bus driver and a couple of students managed to get them separated, there was a generous flow of blood from Jimmy's nose, and Early had a swelling that promised to become a truly classic black eye.

"This time," grumbled the bus driver, "you guys got real trouble."

The dean of boys wasted no time in showing his annoyance with them. "Obviously, neither of you

44

learned anything from your last experience. You, Mr. Plummer, are suspended for three days, And you . . ." He swung his angry glare toward Early. "You, Mr. MacLaren, are placed on campus restriction for an indefinite period."

"R — restriction?" stammered Early. "What does that mean?"

"It means that you cannot participate in any school activities other than regular classwork. No dances, no club meetings, no —"

"What about track?" cried Early.

The dean shook his head. "Absolutely not. Nothing but regular classes."

And right then, Early MacLaren's great day turned into a nightmare. He had to choke back tears as he turned and stumbled blindly from the office.

The dean was not particularly surprised when Ron Canepa called less than an hour later. "Been expecting you, Coach." He glanced at his watch. "Took you longer than I thought it would."

"Listen, Dean, it's about Early MacLaren —"

"Yes, I was sure it was, Ron. I hated to do it to the boy, but I really had no choice."

"But couldn't you punish him some other way?" asked Canepa.

"What do you want me to do, give him more laps? He eats them up like candy. He has to learn a lesson,

Ron, and if this hurts a little then so much the better."

"It's going to hurt him more than a little," Canepa said quickly. "Look, the kid doesn't have much confidence in himself yet. Why — why this could destroy him."

"Oh, I think you're being much too dramatic, Coach."

"Anyway, it's that other boy, that Jimmy Plummer, who always starts it."

"You may be right," admitted the dean. "However, I have several eyewitness reports that the MacLaren boy climbed right over the back of his seat and began hitting Plummer."

"Yeah, but Plummer taunts him," persisted Canepa. "He's always calling him names and he —"

"Okay, Coach," said the dean sharply. "As I said, you may be right. In fact, I suspect you probably *are* right. But I've made my decision and I'm going to stick to it. Now this isn't such an all-fired tragedy, Ron. He'll have to miss the track meet this week, and then we'll review the situation and probably take him off restriction next week."

"Yeah, but —"

"There'll be a lot more track meets this spring. If Early keeps his nose clean, there's no reason he can't run in them."

Canepa sighed. "*If* he runs, Dean. He's a funny kid."

4

THERE WAS a place on the ridge overlooking the farm where a stand of pine trees formed a shelter against the wind, the sun, and prying eyes. On Saturday morning Early sat there for a long time, his thin arms wrapped around his knees. It had been a long and lonely week, and he felt miserable.

He looked up briefly when he heard Billy pushing his way through the thick boughs. Billy hunched down on the soft brown carpet of needles, and for a moment they shared the special solitude of the place.

"What do you want?" asked Early finally.

"Man," breathed Billy. "It's really something up here."

"Yeah," said Early slowly. "Kind of . . . away."

For another moment they stared through the screen of pine needles down to where the farm buildings were a sharp white against the new green grass. From the distance a crow called raucously, its tiny black form flapping hard against the vast sky.

"What do you want?" Early asked again.

"You coming?"

"To the meet?"

"That's it," nodded Billy.

"Why should I? They won't let me run." Early picked up a handful of dry needles and let them sift through his fingers. "Billy, I don't want to be stupid about this thing, you know?" His pale jaw worked a knot in his cheek as he thought. "But sometimes — sometimes it seems everything I do turns out wrong." He wiped his hand along his trouser leg. "I mean — like everybody's kicking me or something, you know?"

Billy regarded him with dark, serious eyes. "Yeah, I know," he said softly. "Sometimes it's like that, but there's not much you can do about it." He shrugged. "You have to stand up to it, that's all. You can't let it put you down, man."

Early looked up then and the sight of Billy squatting there, so serious, so somber, suddenly struck him as quite funny. He laughed and jumped to his feet quickly. "Hey! You must be getting pretty tired of playing nursemaid to a dumb squirt like me. Come on. The coach'll chew you into hamburger if you're late."

Watching a track meet was certainly nothing like being in one, Early decided, as he watched Logan pile up points for a lopsided win over Hatfield High. He couldn't help but think about the great chance for a win he was missing, and he found it hard to get enthusiastic over his teammates' performances. He did, however, cheer with the rest of the crowd when Billy broke the tape in the hundred, the low hurdles, and leaped to a soaring win in the broad jump.

"Three firsts!" said Early with genuine admiration. "Why, you're a hero."

"Yeah, that's me," grinned Billy. "Billy Parnell, boy hero."

The sun was just dropping behind the western ridge when Burdick loped home a winner in the mile, with the closest competitor thirty yards behind.

"Four forty-five," scoffed Billy as he echoed the announced time. "Heck, you could have *walked* it faster than that, Red."

Early laughed. "Oh, sure. Backwards, yet."

Coach Canepa approached, looking as satisfied as a man who has just finished Thanksgiving dinner. "It's time for the relay, Mr. Parnell. I wonder if you'd be gracious enough to go run the anchor leg for us."

"Aw, Coach," protested Billy. "Why don't you give those poor Hatfield guys a chance? They haven't won anything all afternoon."

"Get going, Parnell," ordered Canepa with mock ferocity.

"Going . . . Going," laughed Billy, peeling off his sweat shirt and jogging toward the track.

"By the way, Early," said the coach, "I'm glad to see you out here this afternoon. I was a little worried that — Well, I'm just glad to see you. Enjoy the meet?"

"I'd much rather have been running in it," Early told him.

"Well, I've got some good news for you. I talked to the dean yesterday afternoon and he's taking you off restriction beginning Monday. That means you'll be eligible to run next Friday night when we go over to Jacksonville."

Early smiled at the news. "That's great, but the way things went here this afternoon, it doesn't look as if you need me."

They moved to the edge of the track as the relay began. Logan's third man slipped and almost fell on the baton pass, and by the time Billy got it, the Hatfield anchor man was five yards down the track. Bill's long legs were a dark blur as he caught the opposing runner, zoomed past him, and hit the tape ten yards in front.

"He is *something*," breathed Ron Canepa and then looked at Early once again. "Don't get the wrong idea, Early. This afternoon was a breeze. It'll be very different next Friday night. Jacksonville's got a very good team — and, incidentally, an excellent miler by the name of Tim

Mahaney. We may not do a whole lot of laughing in that meet." He shoved his stopwatch into his jacket pocket. "Oh, by the way, I think I've come up with a solution for your bus problem."

Early looked at the coach with interest.

"How far is your farm from school?"

"Oh, between two and three miles, I guess."

Canepa nodded with satisfaction. "Fine. From now on you don't ride the bus. No bus, no problems with Jimmy Plummer. Right?"

"But my father's too busy," protested Early. "He can't —"

"No father, either. You're going to run it, boy."

"But —"

"Both ways," continued the coach. "To school in the morning, back home at night. No hitching rides, either. Wonderful conditioning for a distance runner. And," he added with a grin, "no problems on the bus anymore."

So Early became a running commuter. He ran to school in the morning, and he ran home each night. And in the afternoon he ran on the school track as Ron Canepa suddenly changed into a real dictator, driving him without mercy. *Sprint!* came the command from the coach's whistle — two shrill blasts. A single whistle — jog awhile. Then, sprint again.

51

It was a long, weary week, but it certainly wasn't a lonely one, and it was good to get back on the track again.

Early sat next to Billy as the bus pulled out for Jacksonville after school on Friday. He set his equipment bag by his feet and settled into his seat as the bus rumbled into high gear.

"Nervous?" asked Billy.

"Naw," said Early.

"Liar."

Early gave a short, jerky laugh. "Okay, I guess I am. Didn't want to admit it, though."

Billy arched an eyebrow at him. "Why not? Man, everybody gets nervous before a meet. I get so nervous I can hardly eat."

Early gave a skeptical glance at the enormous paper bag that Billy had brought along. "Then what's all the stuff in there?" he asked.

"Oh, well, I need to keep up my strength, you know. But I have to force myself," added Billy with a grin.

"Yeah, sure. I'll bet you do."

Someone with a high clear tenor voice began to sing in the back of the bus. Early craned his neck to see who it was.

"That's just Dizzy," said Billy without looking. "He always sings when we go to a meet. I guess that's his way of telling the world he's nervous, too."

"Dizzy Cartwright?" questioned Early with surprise. Dizzy was a mountainous young man who specialized in throwing the shot and discus for Logan. He had two outstanding characteristics besides his great size; an enormous appetite that never seemed to be satisfied — he even came to practice with candy bars tucked inside his sweat clothes — and an equally enormous disdain for physical activity. He was a talented shot putter and discus thrower, but the coach almost had to threaten him with bodily harm to get him to exercise and practice. Now this great oaf was filling the bus with his high and remarkably pleasant tenor voice.

"Now, *he* gets so nervous," confided Billy, "that he can't eat before a meet, either."

"*That* I refuse to believe," chuckled Early. "Hey, Billy, seriously, I want to ask you a question."

"Ask away," Billy said, fishing in his paper bag. "Want a cookie?"

"Listen, what about this guy Mahaney?"

"He's got two legs like everybody else, Red. What else do you want to know?"

"Aw, come on, Billy. I mean is he — is he real good?"

Billy bit into a cookie and looked thoughtful for a moment. "Yeah, he's pretty good, Early."

"Well, I mean — how good?"

"He's good, but you can beat him, Red." He looked at Early with a serious expression. "This has really become a big thing for you, hasn't it? I mean, it's real important to win, isn't it?"

"Well, sure!" Early was surprised. "Isn't that the idea? To win?"

"Of course it is. But the important thing, the really important thing, is for us to beat Jacksonville, you know? And to do that we need a lot of seconds and thirds as well as firsts. In a dual meet like this, you get five points for first, three for second, and one for third. So if we're going to win we've got to —"

"Get the firsts," interrupted Early sharply. "That doesn't take a genius to figure. A first is worth more than a second and a third put together."

"Yeah, but . . ." Billy sighed. "Oh, forget it." His smile was a little forced. "Anyway, you can beat that Mahaney, man."

"Yeah," Early told himself softly. "I can beat him. I can . . ."

But three hours later as he stood on the starting line and half listened to the starter's instructions, he felt far from confident. He looked nervously at Mahaney, tall and dark-haired, with broad, muscular shoulders, slim waist, and long, powerful legs. The Jacksonville ace stood a little apart, with an aloof air, casually raising his arms and flexing his legs. Not once did he bother to glance at any of his competitors.

Finally the starter ordered the six runners to their

marks. Mahaney drew the poll position and Early moved in next to him. Just as the starter raised his gun, Mahaney turned, looked at his pint-sized opponent, and gave an easy grin of confidence. Butterflies careened wildly through Early's body, up and down each arm and leg, and in crazy circles in his stomach. Surely nobody who felt as weak as this, thought Early, could possibly run a mile.

"Get set!" shouted the starter.

The sound of a gun cracked across the stadium.

He ran the only way he knew how to run: just go. Nothing fancy. No strategy. No special plans. Just go, go, and go some more. Early was in front quickly and moving away. Mahaney trailed behind, reluctant to commit himself to such an early pace, but uneasy about the growing daylight between himself and the little Logan County runner.

At first it was something like running across the meadow in the spring, feeling the sweet wind wash against his face. At first it was fun, and it was beautiful. Early could almost make himself believe that he was alone and that the forms along the edge of the track were not human; they were trees and bushes lining his path through the countryside. It was wonderful. A guy could run forever . . .

Passing the half-mile mark. Tim Mahaney knew he was in trouble. That redhead out there was no rabbit.

He was for real. The little legs were chunking out the yards with no sign of faltering. Grimly, the Jacksonville runner set his jaw and stepped up the pace through the third lap.

By the fourth lap the beauty was gone for Early and the pain crunched in his chest as his legs grew heavier and heavier. There was no grassy meadow now, just a long gray ribbon of track wavering before his tired eyes. The air was no longer sweet as it rasped down his throat into his demanding lungs. Despite the pain, despite the weariness, the end was somewhere up there ahead and he would get there — somehow. As he turned into the stretch a blurred form labored up beside him, stayed there for a moment, and then dropped behind. There was a quick, light brush as his chest met the tape and helping hands reached out for him.

Billy's grin almost split his face in two. "Man!" he exclaimed. "You ran. You really ran."

Gulping in air, Early blinked and looked up into his friend's dark face. "I did okay, huh?"

"Okay?" Billy laughed. "I guess you could say that all right."

The tall, dark-haired boy, his face near gray with fatigue, streams of sweat running freely down from his temples, came up and offered his hand. "My name's Tim Mahaney," he said slowly. "I don't even know your name, but that was sure a nice race you ran."

"I'm Early MacLaren."

"Early MacLaren," repeated the boy deliberately. "I'll remember that. I'll be seeing you again in the regional championships." He gave a wan smile. "I'll be ready for you then . . ."

"Early!" Ron Canepa arrived with his stopwatch clutched tightly in one hand. "I just checked with the official timer. Boy, you ran it in four twenty-one and one-tenth. Almost ten seconds better than last time." He put his hand on top of the sweaty red hair and beamed. "And that, my friend, is a new school record!"

5

IT WAS a spring of transition for the red-head from the MacLaren Dairy Farm. As meet followed meet, Early was not only a consistent winner, but the stopwatch told a story of steady improvement. The glory that came with victory was new and heady stuff for him, and he loved it.

Dave watched the change in his son with interest, with pride, and finally with some alarm. As Early embraced a new kind of life, he tended to belittle his old one. A tension grew between father and son, and one warm evening late in May they clashed.

"How come dinner's not ready?" asked Dave. "It is your night to cook, isn't it?"

"Yeah . . . I guess it is." Early waved a vague hand. "I was kind of tired when I got home."

"You were kind of tired," grunted Dave. "I suppose you think I was playing gin rummy with the cows all day."

Early frowned. "Okay, okay. I'm sorry. You can find

something in the cupboard. By the way, Dad, could you lend me a five? I'm going into town with some of the kids."

"You're already into me for ten dollars, and since when do you go into town on a school night?"

"Oh, hell," muttered Early.

"And watch your mouth," snapped Dave quickly.

"Dad, you treat me like I was five years old!"

"Early . . ." Dave made his voice as calm as he could. "We've always gotten along real well, son. I don't see any reason why we can't continue to get along."

"You don't understand, Dad," Early told him sharply. "It's changed. Everything's changed now."

Dave looked at his son with hard eyes for a moment, then turned away to find something to eat.

The next morning, after the milking was finished, Dave drove into school and stopped by Ron Canepa's office. Ron got up quickly and thrust his hand forward as Dave entered. "Good to see you, Mr. MacLaren. You coming down to the state meet this Saturday?"

"Sure going to try, Coach. My hired hand isn't the most reliable fellow in the world, so I hate to leave the farm for very long."

"Well, have a seat," invited Ron. "I'm glad you dropped by." He pushed a newspaper across his desk top. "Just reading an article you'd be interested in. Take a look at Cy Scroggins' column."

CINDER DUST

by Cy Scroggins

Don't look now, but with the state high school track championships only a few days away, little Logan County High School from way up north in the cow country may have just an outside chance at the state title. As usual, Iron City, Roosevelt and St. Mark's will be battling for the top honors, but the word from upstate is: Look out for Logan!

With speedy Billy Parnell logging wins in the sprints, hurdles and long jump, and a ponderous young man named Dizzy Cartwright tossing both the shot and discus blue ribbon distances, the boys from Logan have gone through the regular season without a defeat and strongly dominated the north state regionals last weekend.

The fellow I'm really looking forward to seeing, though, is a jockey-sized redheaded miler by the name of Early MacLaren. Early, a junior, has to get up on his toes to reach five feet and tips the scales at a hundred pounds if he hasn't emptied his pockets.

Lest you big fellows be tempted to laugh, take a squint at the guy's record so far this season. He won the mile against Silver City with a pretty fair 4:31. Two weeks later he whipped Jacksonville's Tim Mahaney with a very good 4:21.1. He made the four-circuit tour in 4:19.5 the following week, and

4:17.8 the week after that. Last week he finished out in front in the regionals with a sizzling 4:15 flat.

Only Ted D'Angelo of Roosevelt and Russ Van Patten of St. Mark's have topped that mark this year. And, of course, the state record of 4:09.6, set two years ago, is just waiting to be broken. And broken it will be — if not this year, then surely next, for both D'Angelo and MacLaren are juniors and will be back.

Anyway, this Saturday, I'm going to be out there bright and Early (pardon the word, Ted and Russ), 'cause I don't want to miss that mile run and seats may get mighty scarce.

Dave tossed the paper back on the desk and nodded. "Yes, it seems like all I've been reading lately are sports articles about Early and the rest of your team. That's one reason I came to see you, Mr. Canepa —"

"Ron," said the coach with a smile. "My name's Ron."

"Okay — Ron," agreed Dave. "Frankly, I've come to get your advice."

"I'm afraid I don't know much about cows, Mr. Mac-Laren."

"No, but you do know quite a bit about my son. I'm afraid he's becoming rather a stranger to me."

"Oh? How so?"

"Well . . ." began Dave slowly. "You see, since Early was a baby he's been small. He was a very small boy, and obviously, he's becoming a rather small man."

"Outside," said Ron firmly. "But not inside. You must be very proud of your son, Mr. MacLaren."

"Of course I am — and by the way, my name's Dave. Yes, I'm very proud of Early. I've always wanted him to do something, you know? I mean he never seemed to excel at anything, or even want to. He's been just a fair student and he's never had any special interests." He shrugged. "He never seemed to get much of a kick out of life until this. It's like a dream come true. It's great. Only . . ."

"Only what?" asked Canepa.

"Well, I'm getting a little worried about him."

The coach leaned forward, putting his elbows on the desk top. "Have his marks been slipping? I insist that my boys keep up their grades. If that's —"

"Oh, no," said Dave, waving a hand. "That's not it at all. As a matter of fact, his schoolwork actually seems to be improving. No, what I'm worried about is Early himself — his attitude. Seems like he's beginning to take himself a bit too seriously. Getting conceited, you know?"

Ron leaned back and grinned. "Well, you could be right about that. I wouldn't know. But tell me, Dave, don't you think it's natural? Your son has come out of nowhere to capture everybody's imagination. Track's always been a major sport here at Logan, but now everybody — and I mean *everybody* — is following our squad. Most particularly they're following Early." He laughed. "Instead of being just another student, he's suddenly become one of the most popular kids on campus. Everybody wants him in their club. They want to sit next to him in class or at lunch. Next thing you know, the girls will be trying to carry his books for him."

"You don't have to tell me," said Dave. "For the past few weeks that telephone rings from the time he gets home to the time we go to bed. I even have to take it off the hook so that we can get a little peace and quiet some nights."

The coach nodded. "Well, isn't it natural for him to get a little puffed up with his own importance? I mean, it all happened so fast. It's a little like turning a kid loose in a candy store, isn't it?"

"I suppose it is," said Dave uncertainly. "But a kid can get pretty sick if he eats too much candy all at once. It's beginning to worry me."

"Well, I think you're worrying unnecessarily," said the coach, with a wave of his hand. "You'll see. He'll settle down pretty soon."

Thursday afternoon Early settled down on the soft grass bank next to the track and relaxed in the pleasant warmth of the sun.

"Early?"

He opened his eyes wide enough to squint up at the tall form of Billy Parnell looming above him. "Whassamatter?" he muttered.

"Done your warm-ups?"

"Huh-uh," grunted Early, closing his eyes again.

"Well, come on, boy. You've got to jog a mile and then do some wind sprints. Coach wants you to work on your starts so you can get out in front of the pack on Saturday."

"I'll get out in front," said Early confidently. "I always do, don't I?"

Billy frowned. "Yeah, but there'll be about twenty-five guys in that race, Red. You've never had to start in a mob like that. And they'll be the very best in the state. Why, Coach says —"

"Coach, coach, coach," snarled Early. He opened his eyes again. "You know something, Billy? You're beginning to sound like him yourself. Why don't you just let me take a little nap, eh? I'm saving myself for Saturday."

"Hey, listen, man —" began Billy, but Early's eyes were closed again and he didn't seem to be listening. For a moment Billy stood there, then he gave an angry shrug and moved away.

By himself, Billy began a warm-up lap, reaching out loose and easy with his long legs and letting his arms swing wide and free. There was a casual grace in the way he moved, smooth and effortless. He had completed a half lap when he heard someone call and he saw Coach Canepa beckoning from the discus circle.

The coach was working with Dizzy Cartwright, who had qualified for the state in both the discus and the shot. Though the big guy was getting some pretty good distance with the platter, he was still rather awkward when it came to the intricate footwork that a good discus man must master.

"You remind me," Canepa was telling Dizzy as Billy walked up, "of a hippopotamus on top of a phonograph turntable."

Billy laughed. "Hey, that's pretty good, Coach. I like that one."

"Well, I don't," scowled Dizzy, threatening his teammate with the discus.

Canepa turned away from the weight man. "I wanted to know if you'd seen Early," he asked Billy.

Billy looked at his feet uneasily and then nodded. "He's over on the far side of the field."

"What's he doing?" asked the coach mildly.

"Well . . . resting, I guess."

The coach's eyes flashed wide. "Resting! What's the matter? Is he sick?"

"I don't know," answered Billy. "I don't think so."

"Listen," said Canepa with sudden anger. "You go over there and tell him — Never mind. I'll go myself."

He turned to Dizzy. "You keep working on that foot-work," he ordered, "or one of these days you're going to get those legs of yours tied in such a knot that it'll take a half-dozen men to untangle them."

They watched as the coach began to walk quickly across the field toward the small redheaded figure sprawled comfortably on the grass embankment. "Oh, oh," muttered Dizzy. "I think old Early's going to get it."

Billy's face grew thoughtful. "And it just could be," he said softly, "that old Early *needs* it."

"You sick?" demanded Canepa sharply as he reached the reclining figure.

Early's eyes popped open and he propped himself up with his elbows. "Oh, hi, Coach. No, I'm not sick. I'm okay. Don't get worried or anything."

"I wasn't particularly worried," admitted Canepa sarcastically. "At least not about your health. But your attitude is something else, Early. I *am* getting worried about that."

Early sat up, rubbed a hand across his eyes, and frowned. "What do you mean? What's wrong with my attitude?"

"Well, for one thing, why aren't you out working like everybody else on this squad? You supposed to be special or something?"

"Aw, gosh, I'm tired, Coach. And I'm as ready as I'm

66

going to be so I thought I'd just rest a little, you know?" He flashed a quick grin. "Besides, the sun is nice and warm today. It's full of vitamin C. Real good for you."

Ron Canepa stood there for a moment, his face flushing to an angry crimson. When he finally spoke, his voice was a low, husky growl. "You get yourself and your — your vitamin C up on your feet and you start pounding that track, Mr. MacLaren. That is, if you want to run in the championships on Saturday."

Early got up slowly and their eyes met for a tense moment, then Early turned and jogged sullenly toward the track.

"Well, maybe Papa Dave was right," Ron said to himself. "Maybe we've got ourselves a little problem here — a little redheaded problem."

There was an uneasy silence between Billy and Early as the bus headed south toward the capital on Saturday. Mostly out of habit, they sat next to one another on the trip, but no words passed between them until the bus was moving through the outskirts of the city.

Finally Early asked, "What are you doing?" indicating the scribbles Billy had been making on a small pad of paper.

"Figuring out points we could get in this meet," answered Billy. He looked seriously at Early. "If Dizzy can win the shot and get maybe a third or fourth in the discus, and if I can —"

"If," scoffed Early.

"Yeah — if!" snapped Billy. "Red, don't you care if Logan wins this meet? Don't you think it would be great to be the state champs?"

"Sure I do."

"Not really," said Billy quickly. "Not the way the rest of us do. I think all you really care about is Early MacLaren and the mile. Your mind is right on that four-oh-nine point six and how you're going to break the record, right?"

"What are you getting so mad about?"

"Not mad," replied Billy in a low voice. "Disgusted would be a better word. You know something, man? I think it all came too easily for you. You just came out and started to run, and bingo! Instant hero. The rest of us had to grind it out over the years, working on technique and form."

"Oh, for crying out loud, don't be stupid, Billy. Sure I want to break the record. Sure it's important to me. Right now I guess it's the most important thing in the world." He took a deep breath. "If Logan should win the team title, why that's great. Wonderful. I'm all for it, believe me. But right now it's the mile and that record. Can't you understand that?"

Billy shook his head slowly and they spoke no more.

The state championship track meet took place each year on the first Saturday in June at the huge Capital City Stadium. It was always a colorful spectacle as athletes representing schools from all over the state gathered together. The uniforms were many colored: the dark blue with white letters of Roosevelt, the green with orange slashband of St. Mark's, the gray and red of Iron City, and a rainbow of others.

A great crowd of spectators filled the stadium and many curious eyes sought out the small but much-publicized redhead from Logan County. And Early felt them all.

"Hello, Early." Early saw the green sweat shirt with the name JACKSONVILLE across the chest in gold letters. Lanky Tim Mahaney grinned down at him. "All set to go? Mile's coming up pretty soon."

"All set," said Early, not returning the smile.

"Gonna be a lot of traffic out there." Mahaney shook his head. "Twenty-five runners — that's too many, don't you think?"

Early just shrugged.

"Say, your buddy Parnell really did all right in the high hurdles, didn't he?"

"Oh?" replied Early. "Did he?" He realized uneasily that he hadn't even bothered to watch Billy run.

"Well . . ." The Jacksonville runner looked puzzled. "Luck," he mumbled, and walked away.

The mile — that's the important race, Early assured himself. *That's what these people have come to see.* He could feel all those eyes boring into him, feeding him with a special kind of energy.

"First call for the mile run," blared the track announcer. It was almost time. Early began to peel off his warm-ups. Then the heavy hand of Ron Canepa was on his shoulder.

The coach gave his final advice in a low, tense voice. "It's a big field, Early — twenty-five. Too many, but there's nothing we can do about that. Now that start's going to be rough — lots of pushing and shoving. You watch yourself. Try to get to the front, but if you can't find any room wait'll the jam clears a bit before you make a move. You got that?"

Early nodded absently. He barely listened to the coach's words. He'd heard it all before. The final call came and Early joined the others at the starting line. There were so many runners in the event they had to be placed in two lines for the start. They drew lots for position, and Early muttered angrily as he found himself assigned to the second row.

Next to him was Van Patten, a broad-chested boy with curly brown hair who wore the orange and green of St. Mark's. He glanced over as he heard Early grumbling. "Tough luck, Shorty," he said with a hard grin. "Watch out for that first turn. Gonna be real kinky."

That was an understatement. At the gun Early felt like one of twenty-five sardines that were all trying to get out of the can at once. Everything was knees, elbows and wicked, flying spikes, and he found himself hopelessly caught in the middle of the jam, searching vainly for a lane of daylight.

Frantically, he tried to fight his way to the front through the pack, but there was a sudden thrust from the side and he felt himself falling. A bright flash went off inside his head, like a pulse of electricity, and then pain quickly flooded the left side of his body.

He skidded along the surface of the track, rolled over twice and then pushed himself to a sitting position. The army of runners was already thirty yards down the track and leaving him behind. Not thinking clearly, he struggled to his feet and began to run again. That pursuit was futile, that all possibility of victory was gone did not seem especially important in that moment of time. He only felt the urgent need to continue.

One side of his face ached dully and his left knee throbbed angrily — but he ran. He was dizzy, and the scene ahead was a vague, wobbling blur — but he ran. Scowling savagely, he kept his eyes down and forced himself to concentrate on nothing but the track ahead.

A lap completed. There would be no record for Early MacLaren. No first place. *No matter. What matters is to run, as hard as possible, one foot in front of the other.* Absently, he reached to touch the hot, sticky place on his face. The fingers came away with a bright red smear.

Another lap. Now a uniform bobbed ahead, white and shimmering, jerking up and down with a strange, puppetlike motion. He passed it, and another took its place. Bright red this time. Red like the color of blood on the hands. It too faded behind and was replaced by another . . . and another . . . and another . . .

He crossed the finish line in eleventh place.

On the way home Early sat by himself near the back of the bus, staring morosely at the night-blackened countryside that slipped past. He had rebuffed all advances since the race, pulling bitterly within himself. His wounds had not been serious, but his disappointment was almost too painful to bear.

Ron Canepa came down the aisle and dropped into the empty seat beside him. Up in front, the boys were in a jubilant mood. Despite Early's disaster, the team had gained enough points to finish fourth out of all the high schools in the state, and that was certainly the best that little Logan County had ever managed. The focal point of the celebration was Billy Parnell, who had garnered a first and two thirds on the day, and was accepting both the congratulations and good-natured gibes of his team-mates.

"How do you feel, boy?" asked the coach in a low voice.

"Okay," came the mumbled reply.

"Hurt much?"

"No . . ." Early was silent for a moment. "Coach," he said finally, "I'm — I'm sorry I fouled up that race. You warned me, but . . ." He sighed. "Well, I guess I was thinking I was pretty good." He shook his head. "I don't know."

"Early," said Ron softly, "no matter how much advice I gave you today, it wouldn't have done much good. There were just too many guys hitting that first turn at the same time." He turned in the darkness and looked at the small, sad silhouette beside him. "But I do agree with you. You were getting to think a bit too much of yourself. You know, you're a good runner, Early, and you certainly had nothing to be ashamed of today. Getting up and running the way you did was something a lot of guys wouldn't have done. I was sure proud of you."

"Really?" asked Early uncertainly.

"Yes, really," answered the coach. "But let me say one more thing to you. The desire to be the best — to strive for perfection — is a great one. I'm all for it, believe me.

And if you keep working and improving the way you have this spring, you will be a *great* runner. Not just good — great. But you've got to learn to live and work and play with your fellow human beings. You're one of us, you know, not some new species of man set apart from all others. The sooner you learn that, the sooner you will become great at whatever you do — rather than just good."

Early was quiet for a moment and then turned to speak, but the coach was gone, moving up the aisle toward the front of the bus. "What a long way I've come," Early thought grimly. "Three months ago I was alone and nobody knew me. Now everybody knows me and I'm still alone."

With the bus only a few blocks from the high school, Early picked up his satchel and began to walk slowly toward the front. Suddenly he was next to Billy's seat and he found himself staring into the boy's dark eyes.

"Billy . . ." he said, searching the expressionless face. He hunted words but found none, so he said simply, "Congratulations."

For a moment Billy's face remained blank, then suddenly he grinned. "Thank you, Early," said the deep, soft voice. "And congratulations to you, too."

6

IT WAS STRANGE not having practice after school the next Monday, but though Early was no longer in training he decided to jog home. It had become a habit, and besides, with this the last week of school for the year he had no desire to ride the bus and perhaps tangle with Jimmy Plummer again.

He was in great shape and kept up a good steady pace along the gravel shoulder of the road. The accident during the state meet had left him with some bruises, but he felt fine and had no pain when he ran.

A sound grew behind him, something like a low flying jet plane with muffler trouble, and then a motorcycle roared past him and pulled to a stop fifty yards up the road. It was Dizzy Cartwright, his vast form astride a shining chrome and black beauty. Big Diz wore a white domed crash helmet and a crimson and white Logan High athletic jacket.

"Whatcha doing?" he called as Early came up alongside him. "Man, don't you know the season is over? You ought to take it easy for a while." He punctuated his speech with roaring bursts of his hand throttle.

"When did you get that?" asked Early. "That looks like a fine machine."

Dizzy fished a candy bar from his jacket pocket, peeled it with loving care, and popped the whole thing into his vast mouth. "Hop aboard, Red. I'll give you a ride home."

Early looked over the cycle with admiration. "It's really nice, Diz. How did you get it?"

"My dad lent me the money." The candy bar consumed, Dizzy hunted for more sustenance and produced a cupcake. He took a large bite and chewed thoughtfully. "Gonna haul hay this summer and pay him back. Come on, climb on. I'll show what this thing can do."

Early hesitated and then swung his leg over the machine and seated himself behind Dizzy. After shoving the rest of the cupcake into his mouth, Dizzy adjusted his goggles and chin strap. "Hang on tight, Red," he advised. "This baby really moves out!"

The wheels spun in the loose gravel and then they were on the macadam. Behind Cartwright's huge form, Early couldn't see much of anything ahead, but as he glanced to the side he could see the landscape was just a blur. They must be really traveling.

"Hey, take it easy!" shouted Early, but the words sailed back into their wake.

"I'll show you what this sickle can do," Dizzy called back. "Keep everything buttoned."

They were almost to the farm road when it happened. The motorcycle came over a rise, and directly ahead of them a U.S. Mail car was just pulling out on the road after making a delivery. Coming the other way was a big diesel truck and trailer. There was no place for Dizzy to go, and he was bearing down on the slow-moving mail car at tremendous speed.

"God!" screamed Dizzy. "Look out!"

He did the only possible thing he could; he ran off the road to the right. The cycle shot off an embankment, becoming airborne over the ditch that lined the road, lit on its front wheel on the far side, then cartwheeled wildly. The machine slid along the ground and came to a stop against a fence.

Early's only warning of the approaching calamity had been Dizzy's scream. Then came a sickening feeling as he sailed through the air, the terrible, jarring impact, a crazy spinning sensation, and then nothing.

He awoke to voices, people over him. He was vaguely aware of pain, but it seemed remote, as though it might be someone else's pain. Something was pushing down hard on his legs. Voices. Was one of them his father's? Might be. He tried to see, but nothing came into focus.

With a sudden sharp burst the pain became worse, worse than anything he had ever experienced. Someone screamed. Was it him? The weight seemed gone from his legs now. Somebody was saying, "Easy, easy . . ."

There was white above him. White with something in the middle of it, but he couldn't tell what it was. And a sound. A whoop-whoop-whooping sound. Ambulance, he thought. I'm in an ambulance. Suddenly he was cold. Very cold. Terribly cold. And the whiteness turned dark.

Time passed slowly in the hospital waiting room. Dave looked across to where Ron Canepa was trying to read a magazine and Billy Parnell was staring blankly at the floor. "There's no reason for you guys to stay," he said, probably for the tenth time. "I'll give you a call as soon as I know anything."

"What I can't figure," said Billy softly, "is how come Dizzy just got bruised, when Early . . ."

"Dizzy got thrown clear," Ron told him, though he knew Billy was well aware of the details. "He just hit the grass bank and rolled. Early ended up under the machine."

"That Dizzy," said Billy bitterly. "He should —"

"Hey, hey," said Dave softly. "'Let's not talk that way, Billy. Let's be thankful that Dizzy wasn't badly —"

The doctor entered then, white coated, serious faced. "Your boy will be all right, Mr. MacLaren."

"Thank God," said Ron Canepa.

The doctor glanced at him and nodded. "Fortunately the upper part of the body received little more than bruises. I don't think there's any spinal damage, though it's really too soon to tell. The main damage is pretty well confined to the legs."

"His legs," repeated Dave dully. "How bad?"

"The damage was fairly extensive, Mr. MacLaren. We've repaired all we could at this time. Now I think we'll leave it up to nature for a while. We'll see later if any further surgery is necessary." The doctor wiped his forehead and managed a smile. "Since he's a healthy young fellow I see no reason to expect complications. I imagine we'll have him walking again in time for school next fall."

"Walking?" said Billy sharply. "What about running?"

The doctor frowned. "I know Early's been a fine runner. I wish I could tell you that he'll be as good as new, but frankly I just don't know. There was a lot of tissue damage."

"Yeah, but —" began Billy.

"Billy," said Dave softly, "let's just be thankful that he's going to be okay, eh?" He managed a weak smile. "I'm very happy to settle for that right now."

Early remained in the hospital for a month. Dave visited him daily and Billy, Ron, and Dizzy were frequent visitors. But though the doctors decided against further surgery and were satisfied that he was healing nicely, he could not walk. Gradually, Early began to grow morose and withdrawn, seldom speaking, never smiling.

One afternoon late in the month, as Dave was walking down the hall of the hospital toward Early's room, he heard someone call. He turned and saw the doctor approaching.

"Mr. MacLaren," he began bluntly, "I think perhaps it's time for you to take Early home." The doctor scratched his chin thoughtfully. "Medically, we've done all we can for him here. The remaining damage should be corrected with time and the proper exercise."

Dave frowned. "You're not really satisfied with his progress, are you?"

The doctor sighed and gave a little shrug. "Frankly, no. He's not responding very well to the physical therapy sessions. He can drag himself through the parallel bars, but we haven't been able to get him to walk by himself — even with crutches." He shook his head. "He should be doing better. Actually, he doesn't seem to be trying very hard, Mr. MacLaren."

Dave looked grim. "I'm not really surprised to hear you say that, Doctor. Sometimes he'll hardly even speak to me when I visit him." He looked sharply at the doctor. "What do you think I should do?"

"Well, it could be that once he gets home, you'll see a big change in him," the doctor said hopefully. "However, I think it's important that you have a good physical therapist work with him on a regular basis until his legs are functioning properly again."

"You want me to bring him in here every day?"

"Yes, I suppose that would be the best way, although I —" The doctor frowned. "Listen, I've got an idea that just might work. I think Early needs more individual attention than we can give him here. Do you happen to know Mary Bruce? She lives down in the south end of the county."

"No, I don't think so."

"Big, nice-looking redheaded lady — just about your age, I imagine. Her husband was a doctor. He was killed in an automobile accident a few years ago. Mrs. Bruce was a physical therapist before she was married. A darn good one, too. We just might be able to get her to help you with Early." He looked closely at Dave. "Tell you what: I'll see if I can reach her on the phone. You go on in and visit with the boy and I'll stop by and let you know what she says."

Early was propped up in the bed, staring vacantly at the window as Dave entered. "Hi, son. How's it going?"

Slowly, the boy turned his head to look at his father and gave a slight shrug.

"Doctor says it's time for you to go home," said Dave.

Early blinked but said nothing.

"Well, you *do* want to come home, don't you?" demanded Dave.

"Sure . . ." The word came out softly, like a whisper.

Dave sighed and sat in a small chair next to the bed. It was hard to carry on a one-way conversation. The walls of the room were a pale lollypop green, the air heavy with chemical odor. He felt a headache, vague and throbbing, near the top of his skull.

"Mr. MacLaren?" The doctor entered quickly. "I just talked to Mrs. Bruce. She said she'd come over to your place tomorrow and have a look at Early. She didn't promise anything, but I think she'll help you out." He turned to the bed. "Well, Early, I think it's time to pack you up and ship you home. That sound pretty good?"

"Yeah, fine . . ."

Dave was eating lunch the next day when a station wagon came down the farm road and pulled to a stop in front of the house. Through the open window he watched, his coffee cup poised halfway to his mouth, as a lady emerged from the car. She was tall and slim and moved with an easy grace as she came toward the house. But what caught his attention most of all was the hair — red and bright as summer sunrise.

Only the knock on the door made him realize that he had been holding his breath for quite some time. "I'm Mary Bruce," she told him when he opened the door.

"Oh . . . yes," he said uneasily. "I — uh — I've been expecting you, Mrs. Bruce."

"Well, may I come in?" she asked, the trace of a smile at the corners of her mouth.

"Oh . . . Of course." Quickly, Dave stepped to one side. "It's — uh — a bit of a mess, I'm afraid."

This time she did smile. "I didn't come to inspect, Mr. MacLaren. Just to see your son." She looked around. "Where is he?"

"He's in bed. His room is right down the hall. I'll show you."

"I can find my way," she told him. "I'd prefer to see him alone. All right?"

Dave nodded. "All right." He watched her go, then went to the kitchen table, poured himself another cup of coffee, and tried to read a farm magazine. When Mary Bruce returned about ten minutes later, he realized that he hadn't understood one word of what he'd read.

"I'm sure a great deal can be done for your son, Mr. MacLaren," she said quickly. "Right now his biggest problem seems to be his attitude. He is simply wallowing in self-pity."

"Well, he's had a pretty rough time, Mrs. Bruce."

"Of course he has." Her blue eyes flashed as she

looked at him. "But until that attitude changes, he's not going to get up on his feet. And that's what we want. Right?"

"Well, sure, but —"

"Mr. MacLaren, Early needs extensive therapy. I doubt that a few hours a day will do the job. I'd suggest that you put him in a rehabilitation center, except . . ."

"Except what?" asked Dave.

"His attitude." Mary Bruce shook her head. "He needs to be here, in familiar surroundings. To see his friends. To be with you." She shrugged. "I really don't know what to suggest."

Dave sighed deeply and scratched the back of his head. He looked up at her slowly. "I suppose this is asking a great deal, but would you consider moving in here for a while, Mrs. Bruce?"

"Well . . . I'm not sure that I —"

"Early needs your help very badly, and I can assure you absolute privacy," Dave assured her. "We have a very nice guest room, and it has its own adjoining bathroom. I'm sure you'd be quite comfortable. Or perhaps you have children of your —"

"No. No children," Mary Bruce said quickly. Their eyes met for a moment and then she smiled. "All right, Mr. MacLaren — for a little while." She extended her hand. "It's a deal."

Dave took her hand. "It's a deal," he agreed.

7

MRS. BRUCE left to pick up a few things and was back in time to cook dinner that evening. It was a dinner which Dave professed was certainly the best that had been served on the farm for a long time. Early ate with them, but remained silent in his wheelchair during the whole meal.

After dinner was finished, Mrs. Bruce wheeled the boy over toward the sink.

"What are you doing?" demanded Early.

"Well, you *can* talk," she smiled. "We're going to do the dishes, you and I."

"And just how am I supposed to do the dishes?"

"You're going to dry," she said, thrusting a towel into his reluctant hands. "There's nothing wrong with your hands, is there?"

"I'm tired," protested Early. "I want to go back to bed."

"Certainly," said Mary cheerfully. "Right after we

finish the dishes. Now I'll wash and hand you the dish. You dry it and put it on the table there."

"I don't see why I have to do this," grumbled Early.

"If you're going to spend the rest of your life in that wheelchair, you're going to have to learn to do things in it."

"Who said I'm going to have to spend the rest of my life in a wheelchair?" asked Early angrily.

Mrs. Bruce raised her eyebrows innocently. "Well, you certainly don't seem to be in any hurry to get out of it."

They finished the dishes and Mary helped Early to bed. Afterward she came out and found Dave sitting at the kitchen table. "How about a cup of coffee?" he suggested. "Just made a fresh pot."

"Thank you. I'd love one." She sat down and sighed. "I suppose you think I was rough on the boy."

He chuckled as he filled her cup. "Of course not. You didn't waste any time, though, did you?"

"Well, I think that's the way to do it." She sipped the coffee. "He's quite a boy, isn't he?"

"Yeah, Early's quite a boy — in lots of ways." Dave stared vacantly into the dark liquid in his cup. "He was a very good runner before the accident. His coach thought he had a good chance of setting a new record for the mile this coming year."

"Yes, I know." She smiled at Dave's surprise. "I'm sort

of a sports fan myself. Mr. MacLaren — let me do this my way, will you? I don't guarantee results, of course. Nobody can do that. But no matter what happens, you mustn't give up hope. Early will certainly walk again. And who knows? Perhaps he'll run again, too."

The hot summer days passed, one much like another. In the morning, the sun climbed out of the dusty red horizon into a cloudless sky, but on most afternoons, growing thunderheads striped the distance with vast marshmallow towers. Often the evening brought storms, quick, electric, noisy. The rain, if it came, was brief but intense. By morning all was clear again, the sunrise intruding on a cloudless sky.

For Early the days were much alike, too. They were filled with pain and frustration, and a person called Mary Bruce. From the time the sun rose in the morning until the lightning stuttered through the dark sky at night, she drove him, she harrassed him, she plagued him until he thought he would go crazy. He wanted nothing more than to hide away from the world there in his room, in his bed. But she wouldn't let him.

She instituted a routine of exercises designed to stretch the ligaments and tendons in his damaged legs and help the muscles regain their strength. Each day the exercise routine became longer, more intense, and often he had to clench his jaws to stop from crying out from the pain.

"Now bend your knees, Early." Slowly he bent them.
"Now try to lift your legs. Go ahead, lift them, lift them, Early!"

"Leave me alone! Get out! Leave me alone!"

"Are you all through with that? All right then, we can begin again with the exercises tomorrow. Right now you can get out of bed and use your crutches. Here we go —"

"Leave me alone!"

She urged him out of his bed and encouraged him to move about the house on crutches. Dave rented some equipment and Early spent more painful hours dragging himself along the parallel bars or lifting weights with his legs. Through it all, Mary Bruce was always there, and he hated her. He despised her. He loathed her!

At first the change in Early was slow, but there was a change. The legs were growing stronger and more flexible. As the summer days passed, the improvement came more rapidly. One afternoon he put on quite a dramatic exhibition when Ron Canepa came to visit.

"Come on, Early," she urged. "One more step." She stood just out of reach with her arms extended. The boy's face twisted into a grimace of concentration and pain. As he started forward his right knee began to buckle and Mary Bruce moved quickly to grab him.

"Good, Early," she smiled. "Very good. You took ten steps that time." She turned and nodded at Ron and

Dave, who had been watching Early's tortured effort. "He's really coming along, isn't he?"

Canepa nodded and Dave said, "He sure is."

"Why, we'll have him running that mile again before you know it," she said, reaching out for a pair of crutches. Early tucked one under each armpit and moved slowly from the room.

Ron watched him go, then turned and shook his head. "Boy, what a runner that kid was going to be." He glanced over at Mary Bruce. "Do you really think it's fair to him to talk about running the mile again?"

Her eyes blazed. "Fair? What do you think is fair? To give him no hope?"

"Well, of course not, but —"

"Now you look here, Mr. Canepa," she snapped, a soft curl of red hair drooping over one angry blue eye. "When I came here five weeks ago that boy wouldn't get out of his wheelchair. Now he uses crutches to get around, and you saw yourself that he can actually take a few steps without any support. Are you going to stand there and tell me that you *know* he'll never run the mile again?"

"Well, no, but . . . It's just that it seems to hurt him so much," said Ron uneasily.

"Hurt him! Of course it hurts him. You don't know how much it hurts him!" She stopped and took a deep breath, and when she spoke again the anger was gone from her voice. "As a coach you should know that there's only one way to make those legs strong again — *use them.* As long as they're not used, they'll —"

"Could I say something?" They turned in surprise to see Early standing in the doorway. "Yes, it hurts," he said in a flat voice. "It hurts more than you could imagine. It even hurts when I'm in bed at night trying to sleep. And when Mrs. Bruce came and practically dragged me out of my nice comfortable wheelchair, I hated her. I still hate her."

"Now, Early —" Dave started to say.

"No, it's true, Dad." The boy managed a wan smile. "But I guess maybe I hate her a little less now than I did at first." He swung his glance to Ron Canepa. "As for running again, I don't know. I *do* know that I'm going to try, though."

With a big smile, Mary walked over to Early. "That was quite a speech, young Mr. MacLaren. Now, how about coming out to the kitchen and helping me with dinner? We'll have to whip up something special with your coach visiting."

"Aw, that's woman's work," grouched Early, trying to hide a smile of his own.

"Indeed?" Mary Bruce raised her eyebrows. "And who fixed the meals before I came?"

"She's got you there, Early," laughed Dave. "Come on. We'd better all come out and give a helping hand."

By the time the school year began in mid-September, Early had made considerable progress both physically and mentally. Though his recovery was still far from complete, he could now manage quite well without his crutches as he moved around the house, and used them only when he became tired. But most importantly, Early had regained his self-confidence. There was no longer any doubt in his mind that he would eventually regain the full use of his legs.

Mary and Dave talked it over with Early and it was decided that he should attend classes on opening day. "If you get too tired," Mary told him at breakfast, "you call, and we'll come get you."

"I'll make out okay," Early assured her.

As breakfast was being finished, there was a strange sound in the driveway. Dave went to the window for a look and began to laugh. "I don't know what it is, but Billy's driving it and it does have a license plate."

Billy was at the door a moment later. "Is Early ready to go? I thought maybe I could give him a lift."

"That's mighty nice of you, Billy," began Dave, "but —"

Early got up and walked slowly to the window. "Hey, man. When did you get that?"

"Yesterday," grinned Billy. "A little old, but I'm going to fix it up."

"It's all right," said Early.

"I'll tell you, Billy, it's very nice of you to offer, but I was planning to take him in myself," said Dave.

"Oh, I'll be glad to take him, Mr. MacLaren. And don't worry — I'm a good driver."

"Hey, let's go," said Early eagerly. "I want to ride in that thing."

"Let them go, Dave," said Mary Bruce softly.

Dave looked at her thoughtfully for a moment and then nodded. "Okay, but be careful, Billy, eh?"

"Great," said Early. "Now where are those blasted crutches?"

"I put them with your wheelchair," Mary told him.

"Huh?"

She looked at him with her steady blue eyes. "They're part of your past now, Early. You can do without them."

The boy thought about it for a moment and then smiled. "Right," he said. He turned and walked slowly out the front door.

Dave watched as Billy drove down the farm road and gave a snort. "That's some car," he murmured.

At the kitchen table, Mary stared thoughtfully at Dave's back. "Do you know something, Mr. MacLaren? I think it's about time I became part of Early's past, too."

Dave turned quickly and frowned. "What do you mean, Mary?"

"You know very well what I mean. I mean that you don't really need me around here anymore."

"Hey, now just wait a —"

"Dave, I came here to do a job, and now that Early's walking, that job is finished. I'm going to pack my bags this morning and I'm going home."

"Mary, I . . ." He hesitated and then sat down with a soft sigh. "It's going to seem kind of funny around here without you."

All was in the usual pleasant uproar and confusion of the first day at school. For Early there was the special good feeling of sitting in the senior class section of the auditorium as the high school principal made his welcoming address. Then there were class lists to fill out, books to pick up, fees to pay. He moved from line to line, room to room, performing the annual autumn ritual. It was great. It was exhilarating. And it was tiring.

He was walking down the main hall during the afternoon when suddenly he swayed and had to brace himself against the wall.

"Hey," said Billy, with a worried expression. "You all right, Red?"

Early took a deep breath and then nodded. "It's just the legs aren't in shape yet, I guess. Got to rest a minute. You know something, Billy?"

"What's that?"

"For the first time since the crash, I really feel good. I really feel like everything's going to be okay."

"Sure everything's going to be okay," said Billy. "Why shouldn't it be?"

Early shook his head. "I was really down for a while. I thought — I don't know what I thought. Anyway, it's okay now."

"Anything wrong, boys?" They turned to face the dean of boys.

"Early's feeling a little tired," Billy told him.

The dean looked concerned. "Say, you'd better take it easy, boy. Think maybe you've had enough for today? Want to go home?"

"No, sir," said Early. "I'm fine now. Our class is right down the hall. Room sixteen." The two boys started away.

"Early . . ." called the dean.

Early turned. "Sir?"

The dean's stern features broke into a smile. "It's good to have you back."

"Thank you," replied Early. "It's good to be back."

The enthusiasm of the first day of school was considerably dampened when Early returned to the farm and found that Mary had left. Father and son ate dinner without enthusiasm and in unaccustomed silence.

"Another hamburger?" asked Dave, offering Early the platter from across the table. Early shook his head. "Are they all right? I haven't done any cooking in quite a while."

"Sure. They're okay," mumbled Early. "I suppose I have to fix dinner tomorrow night."

"That's the deal," agreed Dave. "Unless your legs —"

"I'll manage all right. Guess we'll have hash. Wonder if there's a can of it around somewhere?"

"Hash?" Dave looked a bit glum. He stared at the tablecloth for a moment and then sighed. "We sort of got used to her, didn't we?"

"I guess we did," agreed Early. "Besides being a good cook, she was pretty nice, wasn't she?"

Dave looked up sharply. "I once heard you say you hated her."

"I did. I hated you, too. I hated everybody. But if it hadn't been for her, I'd probably still be sitting in that wheelchair — feeling real sorry for myself." He toyed with his fork for a moment. "You know what I think you should do, Dad?"

Dave got up and took his plate to the sink. "No," he replied dully. "What should I do?"

Early looked at his father's back and said very deliberately, "I think you should marry her."

"What?" Dave spun around. "Now that's really a crazy idea. What makes you say a thing like that?"

The boy shrugged and stifled a smile. "Just a thought, that's all."

Later in the evening, as Early was looking over some of his new textbooks, he heard Dave on the phone solidly for about a half hour. This was so unusual that Early got up and walked slowly to the hall. He saw his father, the phone cradled to one ear, leaning back in a chair with his feet propped up on the desk top and a big smile on his face. He heard him saying, "Yes, Mary, if it's all right with . . ."

Early almost laughed at the sight. *Like a big overgrown teen-ager*, he thought to himself. Silently he turned, went back to his room, and closed the door. There were times when a fellow should be left alone.

8

AUTUMN brought its bright glory to the land. The maples turned a mellow orange and the sumac bushes lined the roadways and fencerows with flaming foliage. Less gaudy, but still splendid in pale yellow and deep rusty red, were the stiff-limbed oaks. The crisp air tasted fine and spicy.

On a Saturday afternoon Early walked across the meadow and into the woods, whistling tunelessly as he trudged along with his hands pushed to the bottom of his pockets. He felt especially good on this bright day. The legs were responding very quickly, and life really seemed worthwhile. Even school, something he had never particularly enjoyed, was proving enjoyable this year. His class work was better than it had ever been, and he had never had so many friends before.

He took a deep breath of the sweet air and grunted with satisfaction. Yes, things were good. Of course, there was always Jimmy Plummer . . . Oh well, you couldn't have everything. Besides, it seemed as though he rarely crossed paths with the boy with the twisted face anymore. Even when they did happen to meet, there was only sullen silence. No trouble. He'd heard several kids predict that Jimmy wouldn't finish out the year, some saying he'd drop out before Christmas vacation.

A covey of quail thundered out of a nearby brush pile and drove all thoughts of Jimmy Plummer out of Early's mind. Yeah, life was pretty good, all right. Tonight both Mary Bruce and Ron Canepa were coming to the farm for dinner, and that made things even better. Early liked both of them a great deal.

"I used to run through here," he suddenly said aloud as he moved beneath the brightly colored branches. "Maybe it's time to try again." Surely it wouldn't hurt if he just jogged a little . . .

At first it was little more than a fast walk, but there was no pain, just some stiffness. The sharp fragrance of autumn filled his nostrils, and it seemed to spur him on. He picked up the pace a little, the legs stretching out a bit farther. It was wonderful. It was the most wonderful thing in the world.

And then with savage suddenness, the pain exploded in his right thigh. Early went spinning down toward the ground, a short scream hissing out between his clenched teeth.

Ron and Mary arrived within a few minutes of each other just before six o'clock. Dave met them at the front door. He was obviously worried. "Early went out for a walk a couple of hours ago," he told them. "I can't understand why he's not back. He knew you two were coming for dinner tonight."

"It's almost dark," said Mary quickly. "I think we should go out and look for him."

It was almost an hour before they found him huddled miserably against the trunk of a huge oak tree. "I think — I think I pulled a muscle," he apologized, the beam of the flashlight plainly disclosing the pain on his face. "I was afraid if I walked on it I might make it worse."

Dave scooped him up in his powerful arms and carried him back to the house.

When the doctor arrived, he examined the leg and shook his head. "Am I to understand you were *running*, young man?" He grunted when Early nodded, and turned to Dave. "Well, I don't think there's any serious damage. Appears to be a muscle tear. Heat and liniment will help, but it pretty much has to heal itself." He got up from the edge of the bed and frowned down at the boy. "Let's not have any more of this running nonsense, eh? You're just going to have to be more patient, Early. You should be quite happy simply to be walking this soon."

After the doctor left, Ron Canepa came into the room and sat on the bed. "How's it going?"

"Okay," replied Early, his voice strangely hollow.

"Much pain?"

"No — not unless I move it. It'll be okay, I guess."

"Sure it will." Ron tilted his head to one side and looked intently at the boy. "You do want to run again, don't you? I mean in competition?"

"You know it," said Early.

"Okay, now you listen to me, and you listen good. When this muscle tear heals, we'll work out a training program for you. But we'll ease into it, see? All nice and planned out — nothing haphazard."

"Coach? You think I can do it? You think I can run again?"

For a moment a grim expression flickered across Canepa's face, then it was gone and he shrugged. "I'll be honest with you, Early. I don't really know. But we'll give it a try, okay?"

"Okay," answered Early.

"Good enough." Canepa got up. "Well, I've had a good dinner and we've had a chance to make some plans, so I'll be saying good night. Time for me to go home."

"So soon?" questioned Early.

Ron grinned. "Well, your dad and Mary — I don't think they need a chaperon, do you?" He gave a big wink. "Good night, Early. Take it easy with the leg."

"I will, Coach. Good night."

Early dozed, but the sound of his bedroom door opening woke him sometime later. "Dad?" he called softly.

"Sorry, didn't mean to wake you, Early," Dave said. "Just wondering how you were feeling."

"I'm okay. Mary gone?"

"Yeah. She left awhile ago." Dave stood in the doorway for a moment. "I — uh — was thinking . . . That is, Mary and I were thinking . . . Well, what I'm trying to say is that we've decided to get married."

"Good," said Early quickly.

"You think so, eh?"

"Yeah, I think so."

"Well . . ." Dave gave a nervous chuckle. "That's good. That's fine. Anything I can do for you, son?"

"No. Good night, Dad."

For a while Early lay in his bed staring up at the dark ceiling. "Great," he murmured. "Just great."

The marriage took place on the first Saturday of Christmas vacation. After the ceremony, Ron was supposed to drive the newlyweds to the airport, where they would fly to a week-long honeymoon in Bermuda.

"You sure you've got everything straight, Early?" asked Dave with a worried frown as the last suitcase was loaded into the car.

"Sure, Dad," said Early. "Don't worry about a thing."

Dave sighed. "I've never left the farm for this long before."

"It's only a week," Early told him. "Arnold and I will be able to handle things just fine."

"I hope so," said Dave uncertainly. "Now be sure you check the fences every —"

"Dave," called Ron, "for crying out loud, let's go. That plane isn't going to wait for you. The kid is seventeen years old. He's perfectly capable of taking care of things for a week."

Dave frowned a moment longer, then relaxed and smiled. He clapped his big hand on Early's shoulder. "Of course he will. I know I can rely on him." He climbed into the front seat of the car, beside Mary, and slammed the door. He rolled the window down quickly as Ron started the engine. "And don't forget there are three cows ready to calve any time now. If we get a bull calf I promised it to Mr. Hackmeyer. You call him and . . ."

Ron shook his head and drove rapidly down the driveway. Early stood and waved until the car disappeared around the bend.

For the first two days everything was routine on the farm, but on the third morning Arnold didn't show up at milking time. Early managed to handle things by himself, but it was hard work. By the time he was finished, his legs were aching with fatigue. Then, at midmorning,

Arnold's wife called to say that Arnold was sick and would be unable to work for several days.

Disturbed by the news, Early sat at the kitchen table for a few minutes. Finally, he got to his feet and headed for the door. There were still many things to do, and without the hired hand he would have to manage them by himself. As he left the house, he was surprised to see a bicycle coming down the farm road, and even more surprised to see who was doing the riding — Jimmy Plummer!

The boy got off the bicycle, an ancient, rust-covered machine, and leaned it carefully against the side of the barn. He smiled crookedly and blinked several times.

Early felt his throat tighten. "What do you want?" he asked suspiciously.

"Uh — well —" began Jimmy uncertainly. "I'd like to see your old man."

"My *father's* not here."

"Oh," said Jimmy. There was a hollowness to the sound. "Well . . . will he be back soon?"

"Not until next week," replied Early curtly.

"Oh," said Jimmy again, and for a moment he stood as though uncertain what to do next. "Well . . . I —" Finally he shrugged, took his bicycle, and turned it around. When he tried to pedal there was a grinding sound and the wheels refused to turn. He got off and regarded the machine glumly. "Drive chain's getting worn," he said in a low voice. "Keeps slipping off the sprocket."

"Looks like you need a new chain," observed Early.

Jimmy's laugh was bitter. "A new bike would be more like it. What I really want's a car — not this crummy thing." He frowned. "But I got to get me a job first."

For the first time, Early really looked at the boy. "Is that why you came — to ask my father for a job?"

"Yeah," nodded Jimmy. "I've been looking all over, but no luck. Pretty tough for a kid to get a job around here. Specially a kid with a face like mine." He flipped a hand. "Aw, I don't suppose your old man would want me around anyway, after you and I . . . Well, you know what I mean."

Early watched thoughtfully as Jimmy bent down to adjust the chain. "Do you know anything about cows?" he asked casually.

Jimmy straightened and frowned. "Well, they moo out of one end and give milk out of the other, don't they?"

Early gave a short laugh. "I guess that'll do for a start." He took a deep breath. "I don't know about this. You and I have never been able to get along very well, but, to tell the truth, I do need some help. The fellow who's supposed to help me is sick. I'd call Billy but I know he's got a vacation job."

There was no expression on Jimmy's face. "I won't give you no trouble, Early."

"Well, if you want to take his place until he's ready to work again, I'm sure Dad would be willing to pay you the same wage."

"Okay," said Jimmy immediately. "That's the best offer I've had." He snorted a laugh. "Heck, it's the only offer I've had. What do you want me to do?"

"The milking barn needs to be cleaned out," Early told him, deliberately choosing the dirtiest job he could. "After you get all the manure shoveled out, hose everything down real well."

Jimmy went to work without comment, and after he finished with the barn, Early had him haul hay bales to the feedlot for the cows and then told him to clean out the calf pens.

"We'll have to start the afternoon milking before long," Early said finally. "How about going into the house for a bite to eat first? You hungry?"

"Yeah," said Jimmy with enthusiasm. "This kind of work gets you hungry — once you get used to the smell."

Early made some sandwiches, and as they ate he asked, "What kind of a job are you looking for? Something for weekends or just during Christmas vacation?"

"Full time," replied Jimmy seriously. "I'm not going

back to school." He pushed more sandwich into his mouth.

"Going to drop out?"

A flicker of annoyance showed in Jimmy's eyes. "Why not? All I ever got out of school was trouble, you know? Well, I'm old enough now, so it's good-bye to history and all that junk. I'm gonna get me some money and buy a car and then none of you'll see ugly old Jimmy Plummer anymore. Just his dust." He smiled at the thought.

By the time the cows were milked and fed again and the barn scrubbed down for the second time, the sudden darkness of the winter evening had arrived. "Toss your bike in the back of the pickup," said Early, "and I'll drive you home."

"Say, your old man just went off and left you with this truck?" said Jimmy as they started down the road. "Boy, if I was you, I'd really go out and swing."

"You would, eh?" Early smiled in the dark cab. "The morning milking begins at five A.M."

"Five A.M.," groaned Jimmy. "You mean A.M. in the morning?"

"That's the one," laughed Early. "And I expect you here. In the meantime, shall we go out and swing tonight?"

"Forget it," grunted Jimmy. "I think I'll go to bed

after dinner. Come to think of it, I'm pretty tired anyway."

Arnold's mysterious illness continued, and within a few days Jimmy was handling the chores about as well as the hired hand had ever done them.

"Think your old man might want to hire me steady?" asked Jimmy several days later as he munched on a peanut butter sandwich and watched Early working on milk records which were spread across the kitchen table.

Early shrugged. "Maybe so. We can ask him when he gets back."

"What the heck are all those things?" asked Jimmy.

"Milking records. We keep track of the production of each cow. Then the butterfat content is checked periodically and —"

Jimmy frowned. "What do you do all that for?"

"Well, it's important," Early told him. "You've got to know how well each of your cows is doing so that you can keep improving your herd." He looked up from his work. "You know, there's a lot more to it than just shoving in the food and taking out the milk. Dairying is a science. My dad went to college to learn this business, and he's always reading books and taking new courses."

"How about that," said Jimmy with mild interest. "I didn't think there was so much to it."

Early's eyes narrowed suddenly. "Do you know how *old* Arnold is?"

"Arnold who?"

"Arnold — the guy whose place you're taking. He's older than my dad. He never finished school. And he comes here every day and cleans manure out of the barn, hauls hay to the cows, and keeps the fences in shape. That's about all he does with his life."

"So?" frowned Jimmy. "Why should I care about this Arnold? I don't even know the guy."

"Oh, nothing, nothing . . . I just thought you might find it interesting."

"Oh . . . now I get it," grunted Jimmy angrily. "Look, boy, I get enough preaching from adults. I don't need any from a little redheaded runt like —" He turned away abruptly. "Sorry," he said after a while. "I didn't mean —"

"No, that's okay, Jimmy," nodded Early, getting up from the table. "What you do is your business — nobody else's. Come on, it's time to start the afternoon milking."

Jimmy had a great deal of natural curiosity, and as the vacation days passed, he learned more and more about the dairy business and began to appreciate that it was not a simple operation. "Hey, look, Early," he said one afternoon while studying a production chart. "This here cow's been giving less milk lately. Maybe she's sick or something."

Glancing at the chart, Early shook his head. "Nope.

We're drying her up. In a couple of weeks we won't be milking her at all."

"How come?"

"She's going to calve in a few months. You always dry up a cow before she calves."

"How about that," mumbled Jimmy.

On the last Sunday of the vacation, Dave and Mary returned, looking tanned and very happy after their honeymoon in Bermuda.

"It was wonderful, Early," Mary told him. She winked. "I think Dave missed his cows, though."

Dave laughed and put his arm around his wife. "I did not. Not at all." She looked at him skeptically and he laughed again. "Well . . . maybe just a little." He glanced around. "Everything seems to be in good shape. Did you have any trouble?"

"No, everything went just fine," Early assured him. "Oh, Dad, this is Jimmy Plummer. He's been helping me while you were gone. Arnold got sick the day after you left and I haven't seen him since."

Dave shook his head. "Doggone that fellow. I forgot to tell you about that, son. Every once in a while Arnold gets to thinking he's sick. You practically have to threaten him to get him to come to work. He's no more sick than I am."

"Well, anyway," continued Early, "Jimmy's been

doing a real good job and he'd like to know if you would hire him full time here."

"Oh?" Dave looked at Jimmy curiously. "Don't you go to school, Jimmy?"

"He has been," Early said quickly, just as Jimmy opened his mouth to speak. "But he wants to quit and get a job. He's old enough."

"That so?" said Dave softly. "Well . . ."

"Uh — well, I was thinking about getting a job, you know?" said Jimmy uneasily. "But — well, I don't know. I — I might finish up this year first."

"I'd be pleased to have you on weekends and holidays," said Dave. "However, I do think it's wise for a fellow to get through high school before he looks for a regular job. Why, these days —"

"Dad, don't preach to him," scolded Early.

"Huh?" Dave looked surprised.

"No, he's right," blurted Jimmy. "Your dad is right. A guy should get a high school diploma at least. And that's just what I'm going to do." He sighed. "I hope."

Early turned away to hide a grin.

9

THAT EVENING Dave was sitting in
the big chair next to the fireplace, reading the newspaper,
when suddenly he put down the paper and exclaimed,
"Jimmy Plummer!"

Early and Mary, who were playing a game of chess
across the room, both looked up in surprise.

"Wasn't that the boy who kept getting you in trouble
on the school bus?"

Early nodded. "The same."

"And now all of a sudden he's your buddy? That's
quite a switch, isn't it?"

Everybody at Logan County High School thought so,
too. In the past year Early had emerged from his shell
of loneliness and made many friends, but Jimmy
Plummer was a loner, an outcast. Not only was he without friends, he was actively disliked by a good many of
his schoolmates. When he had announced in his usual
surly manner before Christmas vacation that he was
dropping out of school, there were no tears of sorrow

shed by his fellow students. Now that they saw him back after the vacation, there were a number of dismayed groans.

But this was a new Jimmy Plummer. Something very important had happened to him. He had made a friend. He sought out Early as often as he could, eating with him in the cafeteria, hanging around with him in the halls between classes. The boy's overwhelming attention wore on Early, but he sensed the great loneliness in Jimmy, the almost desperate need for companionship, and he remembered very well how terrible the feeling could be.

"You know, that kid should be black like me," commented Billy one day.

"What?" asked Early.

"Well, he's your shadow, isn't he? Shadows are black." Billy shook his head. "I don't see how you stand him. He follows you around like a puppy dog."

Early shrugged. "Oh, he's okay. He just doesn't have many friends."

"Man, he doesn't have *any* friends — except you, I guess. Ugh!" Billy shuddered. "That guy gives me the creeps."

"Now that's a funny thing for you to say." Early frowned. "Aren't you the one who's always saying you shouldn't judge anyone by what's on the surface?"

"Yeah, but —"

"No, I mean it, Billy. So Jimmy's face isn't very pretty. Are we supposed to make up a whole new set of rules for him?"

"Oh, man! Forget it," muttered Billy as he turned and ambled away.

"What's the matter with him?" asked Jimmy as he walked up.

"Nothing he won't get over." Early forced a smile.

"Oh," said Jimmy blankly. "Well, let's get going or we'll miss the bus."

"You go ahead," Early told him. "I'm going over to the track and jog a few laps. I think it's time I started to get these pipe stems of mine in some kind of shape. I'll call Mary and have her come down and get me later."

Jimmy looked surprised. "Is it okay?" he asked. "I mean, are you supposed to run yet?"

"I'm not going to try and break any records. Just jog a couple of laps, that's all. That muscle tear is all healed up. Coach has me on a training program, but I think we're moving too slow."

"Well — would you mind if I came along?" asked Jimmy uncertainly.

"You going to run? Seems to me that the last time I saw you run, you weren't enjoying it too much."

Jimmy chuckled. "Guess that's so. Maybe it was because you kept going by me."

"Yeah, I lapped you eight times that day," Early recalled.

"Six," corrected Jimmy.

"Eight," said Early with a grin. "Well, come on if you want. I won't be doing any lapping today."

They jogged two casual laps before Early coasted to a stop and announced, "That's enough for today." He was still breathing easily, but red-faced Jimmy nodded thankfully. "I'll build it up slowly," said Early. "By the end of the month I ought to be able to do eight laps without any trouble. Then by the time track season begins —"

"Hey! Just what do you think you're doing?" demanded a voice that startled both boys. They turned and saw Ron Canepa standing a short distance away. Hands on hips, he was watching them with obvious displeasure.

"Oh, hi, Coach," said Early.

"Don't *Hi, Coach* me, redhead!" snapped Canepa. "Who told you to start running again? I thought you and I had a training program all worked out."

"Well, sure we do, Coach," said Early. "But I wanted to try running a little. I figured I was ready."

"Oh, you did, did you?"

"Well, my legs didn't bother me a bit. Honest, it felt good to run a little. Real good."

Canepa frowned. "Legs don't hurt at all?"

"No, sir. I'm sure I'm ready to start running."

Canepa grunted. "We'll see about that. You'll stiffen up a bit by tomorrow. If not — well, we'll see." He jerked his head. "Come on, I'll drive you two clowns home."

"You don't have to do that. I was going to call Mary."

"That's all right," said the coach. "About time I dropped in on the newlyweds." He turned and looked at Jimmy. "And what's with you, Plummer? You going to become a track man, too?"

Jimmy blushed. "Aw, no, Mr. Canepa. Heck, I ain't no runner."

"I noticed that," said Ron drily. "But you do look pretty strong. Ever think of trying out for the field events?"

"What's that?" asked Jimmy.

"Oh, the jumps, the weights, pole vaulting . . . Hey, how about pole vaulting? There isn't one experienced vaulter in the whole school this year."

"Well, I've watched it a couple of times," admitted Jimmy. "Looks kinda tough to me."

"It isn't easy," agreed Ron. "Nothing worthwhile is, my friend. But if you think you might be interested, I'll be glad to work with you on it." He turned to Early. "And as for you, redhead, you and I are going to come to an understanding about this running and . . ."

So in the days of midwinter, Early began to run again.

When the weather was bad or the track was covered with snow, he ran in the field house, but whenever he could, he worked outside. That was where he felt best, even when the wind was bitter and stung against his cheeks, or he had to alter his stride to miss mud puddles or ice patches. It just wasn't the same inside. He didn't get that great feeling that he always got when he ran outside.

Slowly the days grew longer, and the distance Early ran began to lengthen, too. Before long there were others plodding around the track with him, Billy and some other members of the track squad working themselves into shape for the coming season. And suddenly it was March. The track season was officially under way and the great gray sweat-shirted dictator stood in the middle of the field blowing his whistle and scowling in all directions.

"This bunch of hotdogs couldn't beat the girls' junior high school team in Kickapoo, Nevada," he murmured one day during practice.

"We'd be willing to try, Coach," grinned Dizzy Cartwright.

"Take a lap, Cartwright," barked Canepa. "You look like you're carrying a tractor tire around your middle."

"That's muscle, Coach," Dizzy told him. "Solid muscle."

"Get going, Cartwright," growled Canepa. "You're

as fat as a hog ready for slaughter." But despite the outward gruffness, Ron was really quite satisfied with his squad. True, Early was still a puzzle in the mile, and there were weak spots in several events, but generally speaking, this was going to be a strong team. He thought about his redheaded distance runner and his eyes narrowed with concern. The little guy was running easily and without any muscular trouble, but his trial times were way off last year's form. Canepa sighed. Well, the competition would come soon enough, and then they would know the truth.

The night before the first meet of the season, Ron had dinner at the MacLaren house. After the meal, Early went to his room to do his homework and Mary poured the coffee.

"Did you notice?" said Dave as he took a sip from his cup. "The boy's as nervous as a cat tonight. He could hardly sit here at the table through dinner."

"I don't blame him a bit," nodded Ron. "I'm a little nervous myself. By the way, Mary, that was an excellent dinner. Poor bachelor man like me doesn't get fed like that very often."

"Well, I'm glad you enjoyed it," smiled Mary. "And how do you think Early's going to do tomorrow? He hasn't talked about it much."

"I don't really know, Mary. First meet of the season is always a big question mark. This Fairmont team we're meeting isn't supposed to be very strong, but I don't know much about their milers."

"Well, how have Early's times been in practice?" asked Dave.

"Frankly, not the greatest, Dave. But we've been deliberately keeping the pressure off him." Canepa shrugged. "There's no telling what will happen when he gets into real competition again. Guess we'll find out tomorrow. You two going to be there?"

Mary smiled. "You couldn't keep us away."

The day was not a good one for a track meet. The air was cold, the wind blowing in fitful gusts, and great chunks of gray cloud scudded low across the sky. Rain threatened all afternoon but did not come.

The weather did not slow down the Logan squad. In the first event, Billy won the hundred yard dash by a wide margin, with a Logan teammate in second place. So the visiting Fairmont High team fell behind right from the start and never caught up.

With the mile scheduled late in the meet, Early wandered around in his sweat suit, cheering on his friends as they piled up points in impressive fashion. For the first time in his track career, Early found that he really cared about his teammates' performances. Only in the pole vault was Logan unable to make a good showing. Early watched Jimmy Plummer labor manfully, but he had not really mastered the necessary techniques yet. He did manage to finish third, but it wasn't a very great honor since there were only three men entered in the event. Nevertheless, Jimmy seemed quite pleased. His face creased into a smile that somehow didn't seem quite so ugly anymore, and he touched the big red "L" on his jersey with obvious pride.

The mile drew nearer and Early went through his warm-up routine, doing some jogging, bending, and stretching. With the low hurdles finished, it was finally time. Ron Canepa bent over him as he removed his sweat clothes. The coach said something, but it was difficult to concentrate on the words. The cold wind knifed between his thin freckled shoulders, and he shivered. He realized, with some surprise, that he was afraid — not of the competition, but of his own potential weakness. Canepa slapped him on the back and he found himself walking stiffly toward the starting line.

There were six runners in the race, three from each school. Running with Early were Art Thompson and Al Shirley. Shirley was a slim, promising junior with long dark hair that flowed out behind him as he ran, while big, good-natured Thompson specialized in the eight-eighty, but was doubling up today.

Early glanced at the three runners from Fairmont. He knew nothing about them. For some reason they all seemed to look exactly alike in their powder blue jerseys and white running shorts. They returned his gaze, frankly curious, and obviously respectful. It was a bit startling for him to realize that as the little fire-haired runner from Logan, he had a reputation that commanded that respect. Early blinked his eyes several times and turned away, swinging his arms out in wide circles as he walked a few nervous strides down the line from the start.

Since that day back in midwinter when he'd run the first couple of laps with Jimmy Plummer, he'd been thinking about this moment, wondering, calculating, dreaming, guessing. Now the moment was here, and he shivered again.

"Runners to your marks!"

He moved to the line with the others, shaking out his arms for those last-minute kinks and to relieve some of the tension. Lord, it was cold! Should he try to set the pace the way he had so successfully last season, or should he run with the rest of the pack?

"Get set!"

He raised his eyes so he was looking down the track, and when the gun sounded, his uncertainty gave way to pure instinct. He lunged ahead quickly and led the other runners into the first turn.

He was running! His legs picked up the steady mechanical beat of the pace, his arms swinging out and back, loose yet powerful. Behind, the crunching tattoo of the pursuers, and all around a fresh, cold flow of air. He was running again!

Man, I never seen that kid when he was walkin' . . . You're not a freak — Your mother was small and you take after her . . . You like to run? Why aren't you out for the high school track team? . . . Squirrelly Early . . . What do they call you besides Red?

"Sixty-five!" Ron's shout pierced his thoughts for a moment. The sound of following feet had faded somewhat. The others must be dropping back.

Squirrelly Early . . . Did you get to run? Yeah — I lost . . . Early worm gets the bird. Hah-hah . . . What do you do, keep your legs in shape by chasing cows? . . . I like to run . . . Bend your knees, Early . . . Leave me alone . . . Now get out of bed and use the crutches . . . Squirrelly . . .

"Two thirteen!" Halfway through now. No pain in the legs — a little tired, that's all. Not used to this pace. No sound from the runners behind. They must have dropped back a ways. Maybe this was too fast for the first time out. Maybe — maybe a little slower would be better. A stitch stabbing the side now, right below the ribs. Hurts. Hurts pretty bad. It'll go away. Just keep pumping. Long way around this time.

"Three thirty-one!" Too slow. How did that happen? Others must not be very far back now. Yes, there was the sound. Runners closing in. Pick up the pace now. Move out. Push it harder. But, man, it's tough. The lungs are big blobs of pain, the feet chunks of stone.

Why aren't you out working like everybody else? Aw, gosh, I'm tired . . . tired . . . tired . . . You start pounding that track, Mr. MacLaren . . . tired . . . Squirrelly Early . . . Bend your legs, Early . . . bend your . . . bend . . .

Pain, deep and fierce, eating away at every nerve. A tremendous urge to do something — to get somewhere — despite the pain, despite the terrible, terrible weariness. And ahead . . . a line . . . a dim wavering thing that must be reached . . . must be reached . . .

And then brief but comfortable darkness.

"Are you all right?"

The faces above, dim and misty. Like heads detached from bodies. Count them: One was Ron Canepa; two was Billy Parnell; three, Dad; four, Mary; and five was Jimmy Plummer.

"Are you all right?"

They came into focus with startling suddenness. Early blinked his eyes several times and tried to sit up, but a wave of dizziness swept through his skull.

"Are you all right?" The question came for a third time.

This time he did sit up. "Yeah," he mumbled. "All right. Got a little headache is all."

Ron Canepa managed a weak smile. "You had us worried there for a minute."

"What happened?" asked Early.

"You passed out," said Mary softly.

"No — I mean the race. Did I finish?"

"Finish?" Billy laughed. "Hey, man, you won it."

"I did?" Early started to shake his head, but pain surged through it. "I don't remember." He looked up at the coach. "What was the time?"

"Listen to him!" exclaimed Mary. "A minute ago we were all worried about him and now he wants to know —"

"That's mighty important to a miler, Mary," said Ron quickly. "Mighty important." He put his hand on Early's shoulder. "It was four forty-one and three-tenths. Now you'd better get inside and grab a hot shower. It's chilly out here."

"Gee, that's slow," grumbled Early as he got to his feet.

"Slow?" Ron frowned. "Now you listen to me, Early. You're just beginning to get back into shape, and you still made better time than an awful lot of high school milers in this state will ever make. Jimmy and Billy, give this guy a hand to the locker room. He'll get pneumonia if he stays out here much longer."

The boys reached for him, but Early shook them off.

"I can walk," he said with irritation, and the three of them started for the locker room.

"Well, what do you think, Coach?" asked Dave as he watched his son walk away.

"I'm pleased," said Canepa. "Oh, he's got a long way to go yet, but we've got two and a half months to the state meet." A light sprinkle of rain began to fall, and the coach glanced up at the low sky. "His pacing was poor today. He had a terrible third lap and then ran out of gas there at the finish. But it was the first meet of the season and this was a miserable day for running." He nodded again. "Yes, I'm pleased. I think he's going to do just fine."

"Do you really believe that he'll improve rapidly enough to qualify for the state meet?" asked Mary doubtfully. "We shouldn't get his hopes up if he can't do it."

"Well, like I said, he's got a long way to go," admitted Ron. "But, Mary, you had faith that the boy would run again, right? I was doubtful, I'll admit that. As of this afternoon, I'm convinced his legs are going to take the pressure. So now let me have a little faith that he's going to make it back to the top, okay?"

Dave laughed, and they both looked at him curiously. "With all this faith going for him, how can Early miss?"

10

Now THAT there was competition each week to give more meaning to his daily workouts, Early pushed himself harder and harder. And each week it was a little better, the stride a little smoother and more powerful, the time a little faster.

Silver City, Jacksonville, Dalton, Morris Center, St. John's — the season wore on and Logan County High showed that it was the top team in the northern region of the state as it won every meet with ease. Early, too, remained undefeated. Each race he used the same tactic, roaring to the front at the gun and blistering the full four laps, leaving the opposition struggling in his wake. His times dropped consistently through the four thirties and then into the twenties.

Finally the regular season was over, with only the regionals left before the state championships. Ron Canepa, who was a frequent visitor at the MacLaren farm, stopped by on Wednesday night for dinner.

After dinner, Ron and Mary sat down on the porch

to what had become a regular chess match. Mary was very good at the game and Dave didn't play, so Ron volunteered to provide the opposition while Early went to his room to do his homework.

"You're not playing very well tonight, Coach," said Mary.

"Guess not," agreed Ron. He got up and stretched. "A fella can get whipped just so often before he begins to lose heart." A large buff-colored moth beat its wings against the porch screening, and the serenade of frog and cicada came out of the darkness of the warm late May evening.

"No, it's more than that," she said gently. "Your mind is off somewhere else this evening."

He grinned at her. "You're right. All I can think of is that regional qualification meet over at Jacksonville this Saturday and then the state meet at the capital the next weekend."

Dave looked up from his newspaper. "Been hearing some talk about little Logan taking the state championship this year. Any chance, Ron?"

"Oh, I don't even want to think about that," said Ron. "We'll do all right in the regionals. Should qualify ten or twelve boys. But the state — that's something else."

He locked his arms behind his back and squinted thoughtfully through the screen. "Roosevelt has an awfully good team, as usual. And Iron City is supposed to have one of its better squads." He sighed noisily. "Still, if Billy can win the high hurdles and the broad jump, and maybe grab a third or fourth in the hundred . . . And if Dizzy can —" He gave a short, harsh laugh. "Dave, I just don't know."

"How about Early?" asked Mary carefully. "Can he win the mile?"

"Who knows what the kid can do? He was under four twenty the last time out. He'll breeze in the regionals. There's nobody in the north region who can come near him. But the state'll be something else. That D'Angelo kid from Roosevelt ran a four-ten flat last week. He's a great one."

The telephone rang inside the house and they heard Early call, "I'll get it."

"Say," said Ron with a nod of his head, "the redhead's been doing a lot better with his schoolwork lately, hasn't he?"

Dave smiled and pointed a finger at Mary. "You can credit *that* redhead for some of it. She's really been working with him."

"Well, he can't run the mile for the rest of his life," observed Mary. "He wants to go to college, and I've tried to impress upon him that he needs good grades."

"Listen, if he wins the state title in the mile, there should be a couple of dozen colleges clamoring to get him."

Early appeared in the doorway. "Phone call for you, Coach."

"Oh, thanks. I left your number at my rooming house," he told Dave. "Probably some irate parent wants to know why I overworked their fat little darling in P.E. today."

When he turned about five minutes later, Dave asked, "Irate parent?"

Ron shook his head and looked thoughtful. "No . . . It was Jed Masters. He's the assistant athletic director at Parker University."

"Gee, what did he want, Coach?" asked Early.

"Early, that's really none of our business," chided Mary softly.

Ron sat in an easy chair and waved his hand. "I don't mind telling you. The head track coach at Parker is retiring at the end of this season and I put in my application for the job."

Dave whistled softly. "Hey, Parker — that's big time, Ron. Parker is a fine university."

"Do you think you'll get the job, Coach?" asked Early.

"Well, I didn't think I had a chance," admitted Ron. "I know they had a large number of applications for the job. And some of them are outstanding men." He couldn't suppress a grin. "But Masters just called to tell me that the athletic advisory board has narrowed the field to five candidates — and I'm one of them."

"Hey, that's great!" said Early.

"Congratulations, Ron," said Mary.

"Wait a minute!" protested Ron. "I'm just one of five. There's another college coach, two junior college coaches and Johnny Gleason, the head man down at Roosevelt High, still in the running. And Masters more or less admitted the board is sort of leaning toward Gleason. He's got a fine reputation."

"When are they going to decide?" asked Early.

"They're going to wait until after the state meet," Ron told him. He jumped to his feet and began to pace the porch. "You know, if we could just take that state title, then I'll bet —" He gave a short laugh and looked around, embarrassed. "There I go again with that *if* business, eh? But, doggone it, it's the chance of a lifetime."

"Oh, I do hope you get it, Ron," Mary told him. "Parker's a wonderful place." She glanced over at Dave. "I wish Early could go to a place like that."

"Parker's mighty expensive," grunted Dave. "With all the medical expenses and everything, we'd have a pretty tough time swinging it, I'm afraid."

"Well, they give track scholarships, you know," said Ron. "The boy has to be both an outstanding track man and a good student. The way Early's schoolwork has been improving, I'm sure they'd give him strong consideration. They've already expressed interest in Billy Parnell. Why, if I got the job and if Early won the state title in the mile —"

Mary laughed and Ron blushed. "I'm doing it again, aren't I?" He looked at Early and tilted his head a bit. "I think maybe you and I had better just concentrate on this regional meet for right now. Right?"

Early smiled. "Right!"

The state was divided into five regions for the qualifying meets, and on Saturday track men from high schools in the northern part of the state descended upon Jacksonville. The Logan County crew was loose and confident. As they got into their uniforms in the crowded locker room, Dizzy had some free advice for the unbeaten miler.

"Just get out in front, Red," he said through a large wad of bubble gum. "And don't let nobody pass you. That way, you can't lose."

"Thanks a lot, big man," grunted Early. "I'll sure try and remember that. Now here's some advice for you. Just throw that oversized BB you play with farther than anybody else and *you* can't lose, either."

"You don't *throw* a shot," scowled Dizzy. "You *put* it."

"Put it where?" asked Early with an innocent smile.

"Put *what* where?" asked Billy, joining the group.

"Did one of you guys lose something?" asked Jimmy Plummer.

"Aw, you guys," muttered Dizzy, pivoting his vast bulk with surprising agility and stalking away in disgust.

After the boys were dressed they left the locker room and gathered in a group near the track. "I just want you guys to remember," Ron Canepa told them, "that today a fifth is as good as a first. The first five places in each event qualify for the state meet and getting qualified is the important thing today."

Early kept his warm-ups on despite the heat of the afternoon sun. With the mile scheduled late in the meet, he ambled around from event to event, cheering as Billy won the high hurdles and finished second in the hundred yard dash, as Art Thompson took a solid third in the eight-eighty, as Dizzy Cartwright scored easy victories in both the shot and discus. And then there was the moment when Jimmy Plummer, all muscle and desire with very little form, struggled over the pole-vault bar to earn a fourth place.

"You did it!" shouted Early slapping his open hand. "Way to go!"

Jimmy's smile was huge. "Well . . . a fourth . . . I didn't exactly set no records."

"Fourth is as good as a first," said Billy Parnell, coming over to add his congratulations. "You heard Coach say so."

"Yeah . . . well, at least I get to make the trip next week, huh?"

And when it was time for the mile, Canepa eyed his little runner anxiously. "Remember what I said about qualifying, Early. Stay out of trouble out there. No knockdowns or anything like that. Just hang in there and finish in the top five, okay?"

Early looked up with wide blue eyes. "I like to finish first, Coach. I'm just going to get out there in front and try and stay there, like I usually do."

"I know, I know," said Canepa. "I'm just trying to tell you that it may not be that simple, Early. They know you're a fast starter and they'll be —" He waved a hand in exasperation. "I don't know why I even bother talking to you before a race. You hardly ever listen, and even when you do, you never do what I tell you."

Early blinked twice and managed an innocent smile. "I try, Coach. Honest I do."

Canepa rolled his eyes skyward and walked away.

At the gun, a half dozen runners struggled to beat Early to the first turn, and three of them did. Careful to avoid potentially dangerous contact, Early decided to slide over to the poll when he saw an opening and be content with fourth spot for a while. He would make a move in the backstretch, he thought, just as soon as the traffic thinned out. But as they moved out of the turn, he found a runner loping along right beside him and he didn't have to look over his shoulder to feel another runner right behind him.

"Oh, oh . . ." said Art Thompson as he watched the race.

"What's wrong?" asked Jimmy Plummer.

"He's boxed," said Thompson. "They've got him trapped, can't you see? A guy behind him, another in front and one to the outside. He can't get out."

"Oh . . ." said Jimmy. "But they can't do that, can they?"

That's what Early was thinking, too, but they not only could, they were. He was wrapped up as neatly as a Christmas package. Whether all these runners from different schools had actually planned this strategy, Early would never know, but he realized that now they had him boxed, they were not about to let him go.

Early fumed through a seventy-three-second first quarter and a two twenty-eight half. The men around him, he knew, were in no hurry. If they could, they would keep him boxed in until they were within sprinting distance of the finish line, and then they would see if they could beat him home. And what made it especially bad, he realized, was they just might get away with it.

By the third lap, Early's anger was gone and he had developed a plan of action. Just as they moved into the first turn of the third lap, Early slowed abruptly. The man on the outside also slackened his pace in order to keep him covered, but the runner directly in front of him began to pull away, and this opened a lane of daylight to the front and left. Immediately the redhead shifted into high gear, sprinting clear of the box before the lid could be slammed down again. Without slacking his pace Early tore by the three runners who had been out in front, blistered down to the second turn and around into the final lap.

"If they want to beat me, they'll have to catch me," he thought grimly. He floated a bit during the first half of the last lap, but then he turned on the burner again for the last two hundred yards and romped home thirty yards in front.

"Good going, Early," smiled Ron Canepa. "Had me worried there for a while, though." The coach was jubilant. "Well, we qualified twelve men for state. Roosevelt — Iron City — you'd better look out!"

That evening, after returning home, Ron placed a person-to-person call to Jed Masters at Parker University.

"Hey, Ron, how's it going? My wife and I were just going out the door when you called."

"Well, listen," apologized Ron, "I don't want to hold you up. You go —"

"No, no," said Masters. "That's all right. What's on your mind?"

"I was sort of wondering if there was anything new on the coaching situation?"

Jed Masters chuckled. "I thought it might be something like that. I can't tell you anything officially, Ron — but off the record, the athletic board has pretty well narrowed it down to you and Johnny Gleason."

"Is that right?" Canepa felt a little thrill shoot through his body.

"As I told you earlier," continued the assistant athletic director, "we plan to announce our decision right after the state meet on Saturday. Oh, by the way, while I'm thinking of it: The Parnell boy's scholarship has been approved. I'm mailing out formal notification on Monday."

"Hey, that's great," said Ron. "Say, Jed, I've been meaning to talk to you about Early MacLaren. I think he —"

"Oh, that's your little miler, isn't it? Must be a real gutsy little guy. Sort of small for college competition, though. Did you know that Ted D'Angelo of Roosevelt has signed a letter of intent with us? He's going to be a great one."

"Yeah, but —"

"Listen, Ron, I hate to cut this short but the wife is getting kind of impatient. We are late for a dinner date. We'll be seeing you on Saturday, right? And good luck, boy."

11

The track was long and twisted through the woods in alternate patches of sun and shadow. The sound of a hundred feet beating its surface, somehow staying in thunderous cadence, made the air vibrate. He tried to fight his way between the flailing arms, the flying feet with their shark-teeth spikes, but it was impossible. It was like swimming in applesauce. And still the world was bright and dark and bright again in rapid succession. Suddenly he was falling, spinning slowly toward the earth, arms braced for impact, mind cringing in the anticipation of the quick, savage pain. But there was only darkness.

Darkness . . . A quick pulse of light threw dim shadows across the room and a stirring breeze made the window drapes reach inward like a pair of ghostly arms. In the distance thunder rumbled.

Early took a deep, deliberate breath and let it out slowly, forcing his clenched fists to open and relax. After a moment, he got out of bed and walked to the window, still shaken by the dream. Lightning streaked down the sky off in the east and the air was rich with the smell of wet grass and leaves.

Sleep, he decided, was remote now, so he stepped out into the hall and walked through the dark house toward the kitchen, the floor cool and pleasant against his bare feet. After turning on the kitchen light, he poured himself a glass of milk and sat at the table. The last evening's newspaper was there; he flipped to the sports page and began to read Cy Scroggins' column for the third time . . .

CINDER DUST

by Cy Scroggins

Tomorrow's the big day for high school track and field men as the state championships are held at the capital. Rumors still persist that Johnny Gleason will be named the new head coach at Parker University right after his heavily favored Roosevelt High squad grabs the team title.

Highlight of the meet should be the mile run, where the brilliant Ted D'Angelo is given an excellent chance to set a new state record. Despite a strong field in the event, no other miler is expected to give D'Angelo much of a —

"Early MacLaren, what are you doing up this time of night?" Mary stood in the doorway, wrapped in a blue terry-cloth bathrobe and with fluffy pink slippers on her feet.

Early looked at her and smiled weakly. "Couldn't sleep. Join me in a glass of milk?"

She walked to the table and nodded. "You know, of all nights not to get your sleep, this is a bad one."

"Yeah," agreed Early. "Going to be a long day." He stretched and yawned. "Too much on my mind, I guess. Can't turn it off. Oh, I slept some." He shook his head and snorted. "But there were some pretty wicked dreams."

"Do you feel all right?"

"Sure," said Early easily. He stared into the glass of milk for a moment and then he looked up at Mary. "Funny, isn't it? I mean how it all comes down to this. It seems as though my whole life has been leading up to this meet tomorrow."

Mary smiled. "You mean *today*. It's two o'clock in the morning."

"Hey, you're right. It is."

"Well, it certainly will be a big moment in your life, Early, but I'm sure there will be a great many more such times. You have a great future ahead of you."

He shook his head again. "Sorry, Mary, I just can't

see beyond this meet. Whatever the future, it's going to have to wait."

The Logan boys were unusually quiet on the trip to the capital. The school bus clicked off the long miles monotonously, cruising past the dairy farms of the north country. The towns grew bigger and busier: Kirtland, Franklin, Iron City. The rolling hills gave way to the broad central plain, and finally the skyline of the capital loomed ahead.

"I wonder what's wrong with Dizzy," said Early. "He's not singing today."

Billy shrugged. "He's uptight like everybody else, I guess." He glanced toward the front of the bus, where Ron Canepa was sitting by himself. "Now *there's* a fella who's really struggling."

Early nodded. "Sure hope we can pull it out for him."

The corner of Billy's mouth curled up slightly. "What d'you mean for him? Man, track is an individual sport, don't you know that? Where you been, boy? It's everybody for himself out there today."

"Oh, shut up," grinned Early. "Honestly, what do you think, Billy? Can we take Roosevelt?"

Billy shrugged, his face serious. "Going to be tough, Red. Going to be mighty tough."

Roosevelt showed just how tough they were going to be early in the meet. Billy whizzed home first in the high hurdles, but blue-shirted Roosevelt runners took second and fourth. With a fine effort, Art Thompson finished fourth in the eight-eighty, but a Roosevelt runner was up in second. Despite his defiance of almost every rule of good form, Dizzy skimmed the discus farther than he ever had before. The effort was good enough for a third, and, sure enough, there was a Roosevelt man right behind him in fourth place.

"How's the team score going, Coach?" asked Early.

"Close, boy, close. Looks like this thing is going down to the wire."

"Say, I know you don't like to see me in a horizontal position, but I didn't sleep very well last night and the mile isn't coming up until the last event. Do you mind if I go into the locker room and rest for a while?"

Canepa glanced at his miler with a worried frown. "You feeling all right?"

"Sure, I'm fine. Just a little tired, that's all."

"Okay," nodded Ron. "You go on. I'll come get you when it's time to warm up."

Through the afternoon, Canepa moved from event to event, keeping track of the team score, giving advice and a helping hand when necessary, cheering and groaning at his boys' efforts. Billy was out of the blocks late in the hundred and didn't place — a few points that had been counted on were gone. Then Jimmy Plummer got an unexpected fifth in the pole vault — a point gained back. Billy made up for his failure in the dash by winning the broad jump with a leap that missed the state record by only three inches.

It was still close — too close to figure. Ron sighed heavily. "Well," he muttered to himself, "however it ends up, I'm proud of them."

"And you should be," said a voice.

Canepa turned quickly and saw the tall, muscular form of Jed Masters standing beside him. Masters, once an all-American football player for Parker, was ruggedly good-looking. He wore his blond hair long and carefully groomed, and an unlit pipe was clamped firmly in his big jaw.

Masters gave him an amused glance. "You know, you don't exactly look like the picture of the proud coach right now, Ron."

Canepa managed a strained smile. "I'm in the process of dreaming the impossible dream, Jed, and it's beginning to get on my nerves." He glanced at his watch and exclaimed, "Hey, it's getting close to the mile. I've got to make sure Early gets warmed up. Excuse me, Jed."

Masters removed his pipe and stood for a moment watching the Logan coach hurry away. "Hey, Ron!" he called. "Hey, I wanted to tell you . . ." But Canepa was already out of hearing range.

Early had been dozing on a bench in the locker room when he heard the voice: "Better get up. It's almost time." He opened his eyes and recognized the dark, handsome face of Ted D'Angelo. The Roosevelt miler sat down beside him and sighed. "Be all over pretty soon."

Early blinked his eyes several times and then sat up. "What time is it? I must have been sleeping."

"Yeah, you were," agreed D'Angelo. "It's almost time to run. I saw you snoozing here and figured it was time for you to wake up. Want to go out and jog a lap or two?"

"With you?" asked Early in surprise.

"Sure, with me," laughed D'Angelo. "What's the matter, am I poison or something?" He extended a long, thin-figured hand. "By the way, I'm Ted D'Angelo."

"I know," said Early, shaking the hand. "I'm Early MacLaren."

"I know," grinned D'Angelo. "How about you and I go out there and break that mile record, eh?"

"Give it a shot," agreed Early. "If I can just make it to that first turn without getting totaled. Man, I hate that traffic at the start."

"Yeah," said D'Angelo. "It's rugged. All you can do is play it cool and pick your spots." He slapped Early's scarred knee. "Well, the folks are waiting for the mile 'cause that's the glory race. Let's go give it to them."

They were just leaving the locker room when they met Ron Canepa. "Better get warmed up, Early. The mile's coming up in a few minutes. Everything okay?"

"Right," nodded Early. "Had a little nap. How are we doing?"

Canepa's expression betrayed no emotion. "We're doing all right. Now don't you worry about that. You just concentrate on the mile."

The coach watched as Early and Ted D'Angelo crossed the track and sat on the grass to put on their shoes. The late afternoon sun threw the long shadow of the grandstand across the infield area. The crowd noise and the merry-go-round of athletes swept around them unnoticed as they went through their warm-up routines. Canepa had considered telling Early the truth — that only a Logan win in the mile could give them the team title. Johnny Gleason's Roosevelt squad was carrying a slim one-point lead into this final event. But he'd decided to let the redhead go into this race without the extra pressure on his back.

"Ladies and Gentlemen," boomed the announcer on the public-address system. "Your attention is called to event number eighteen on your program — the mile run. This is the final event of the meet. Entries in this event are —"

Early found himself surrounded by his teammates now — Billy, Jimmy, Dizzy, Art — all of them slapping his shoulders, grabbing his hand. "Good luck, man." "Go get 'em, Red." "You can do it, Early."

"Hey!" shouted Early. "What about the team score? Have we got a chance to win it?"

Billy gave a weary shrug. "Don't know. It's pretty close, Red."

Early was assigned a front-line position and dropped into a sprint start. The starter raised his gun and began the ritual chant: "Runners to your marks!" Early felt his muscles tense; "Get set . . . . . ." And then the gun's report echoed across the stadium. It had begun!

He went with the gun, starting the four laps as though the race were the hundred yard dash. A number of others had the same idea, but Early beat the crowd to the first turn, and by the time they came out into the backstretch, he had the poll and the lead. Despite the large field of talented runners, it became quickly apparent that this was to be a classic two-man battle. Early was setting a blazing pace out in front, with the graceful form of Ted D'Angelo floating right behind him. A rapidly growing gap of daylight showed between these two and the rest of the pack.

Canepa felt the tightness build inside his chest as it always did when he watched one of his boys in tough competition. For the moment, thoughts of the meet score, of Johnny Gleason and Roosevelt, and the Parker University job all faded into the background as he felt himself out there running in the redhead's shoes. He could almost feel the great gulping need for oxygen in his lungs, hear the soft, eager crunch of the pursuer's stride, feel the menacing shadow over his shoulder.

Through the first lap and into the second, the pace remained the same, the two front runners locked together as though paced by a drumbeat they alone could hear. Discouragement was already evident on the faces of the other runners as they struggled to cope with a challenge that was beyond their capabilities.

"Little guy can really go, can't he?" The rumbling voice was Jed Masters' again, but Ron could not tear his eyes from the track. "Maybe you were right about him, Ron. If you want him at Parker with you, I'm sure it could be arranged."

Suddenly, Canepa realized he had not breathed in quite a while. He took a deep breath and forced himself to turn and look at the big man. "What are you talking about?"

Masters gave a huge smile. "What I was trying to tell you earlier, but you got away from me. You're the one they picked. The athletic board has decided to offer you the head coaching job at Parker next year."

Ron opened and closed his mouth several times before any words came. "But we haven't won this thing yet. If we don't take the mile —"

"That has nothing to do with it, Ron. You were actually selected several days ago, but the board wanted to wait until after the meet to make the announcement."

"But I thought —"

Clamping a vast hand on Canepa's shoulder, Masters said, "You've done a great job up at Logan County and I know you're going to do a fine job at Parker."

A sudden rise in the crowd noise drew Ron's attention back to the track. Guilt mixed with elation as he realized that for a few moments he had forgotten about Early struggling out there against that long-strided runner.

D'Angelo made his move at the start of the third lap. Early heard the footsteps suddenly grow louder, and then the blue-shirted figure moved by him. The tactic was not unexpected. It was D'Angelo's habit to follow the pace for the first half mile if it was fast enough to suit him, then move to the front with a sharp burst of speed. From then on it was "Catch me if you can," and for the past two years no one had been able to overtake the Roosevelt ace.

"There he goes!" cried Masters. "Your little fellow will never get him now."

"We'll see," said Ron grimly. Once again all other thoughts had been banished, and the coach was mentally back out there on the track, urging on his runner. He had hoped that if Early could set a fast enough pace for the first half mile, D'Angelo would not be capable of making his traditional third-quarter charge. The great Roosevelt runner had just dashed those hopes. Now it was all up to Early and that vague, immeasurable quality down deep inside the small freckled body, commonly known as guts.

Early was determined not to let D'Angelo get away from him. He willed an increase in speed. Somehow his body responded, and he clung close to the flying heels ahead. Out of the second turn and into the straightaway, the Roosevelt boy felt confident enough to ease up slightly. This was what Early had been waiting for, and he pulled alongside the surprised D'Angelo. As they crossed the line and moved into the final lap, Early had regained the lead by a slim stride.

From the crowd jammed along the edge of the track, Billy's dark face, filled with excitement, suddenly stood out. "Go, Early!" he screamed. "Give it all you got, Red!"

Through the fourth frantic lap the two runners held together like a body and its shadow. Form was gone now, and with it tactics and finesse and all the nice things about running. Now it was a test of animal energy, of bone and tissue and muscle, of the ability and willingness to call upon all the resources of stamina these two fine athletes had stored in their bodies.

Give it all you've got. Like pulling the stopper out of a bathtub. Until there's nothing left . . . Everything you've ever worked for, ever fought for, is here in this race . . . Now . . . There's nothing before it. Noth-

ing after it . . . Now . . . Everything you've got,
Early . . . Everything . . .

The pain that blossomed in his small body was like a flame of pure agony. But he was no stranger to pain. Pain was simply a matter of the mind. It was something to be endured. Endured, it went away — eventually. And still the great hovering presence of D'Angelo clung to him like a thing attached.

The turn. The final stretch. The roar of the crowd. *Faster! Faster! Give it all you've got!*

But he had given all. There was nothing left — only the soft, almost unfelt sensation of the finish tape brushing his chest. And then the world spun wildly around.

"Hey, how about that," muttered Jed Masters. "Didn't think he could do it." He turned to Canepa, but the coach was already hurrying toward his runner. "Hey, Ron!" he called. "Just think what it's going to be like working with those two kids for the next four years, eh?"

Ron pushed his way through the mob surrounding Early and wrapped his arms around the boy's heaving shoulders with a hug of elation. "Great, Early," he shouted. "Just great. I think —"

"Ladies and Gentlemen," interrupted the public address. "Here are the results of event number eighteen, the mile run. The winner was MacLaren of Logan

County High School. The official time of the race was four minutes eight and six-tenths seconds, breaking the old state record of —"

The crowd roar surged up to overwhelm the rest of the announcement.

"You hear that?" cried Ron. "You did it! You broke the record!"

In the swirling crowd of well-wishers, Early found D'Angelo and grasped his hand. "Good race, Ted. Really good."

D'Angelo managed a weary but genuine grin. "But not quite as good as yours, Early. Congratulations."

Someone pulled him away. Flashbulbs popped in the early evening light. There were questions and more questions, and a microphone was thrust at him.

"Isn't that something?" observed Billy.

"Sure is," agreed Dizzy.

"Seems hard to believe," said Jimmy, "but I knew that guy when he was nothing more than a pesky little runt on the school bus — always gettin' me in trouble." He shot a crooked grin at Billy. "You know, that kid has come a long way since then."

For a moment Billy looked at him with dark, serious eyes, and then he smiled. "Man," he said softly, "we've all come a long way since then."

They turned and took the shortcut back to the locker room.